"The Hollow Soul"

A Fictionalized Novel
Of A Political Game

By Marilyn Wright Dayton

Jill –
Here it is –
my very first
fictional novel –
the written from 30 years
almost
ago – Enjoy –
Marilyn

2nd Printing

Copyright © 2021 Marilyn Wright Dayton

ISBN: 9798721521751

DEDICATION

I would like to dedicate this book to all of the Native American
Indian Nations who have fought so
bravely to keep their traditions, their rights and their land.

The Hopi Nation is one of the oldest civilizations in America.
*"The Hopi People speak not as a defeated little minority in the
richest and most powerful nation on earth, but with the rising voice
of a people affirming their rights to grow from
their own native roots."*

This is a fictional novel, but the sources for the Hopi Nation
references and information give us real information
about this ancient tribe.

The references and information on our political system in the
United States are from reputable sources, so consider the
information in this book what you will.

This book was originally written in 1993, but I was asked by
several publishing companies to rewrite it to their liking. I was not
ready to do it at that time.

As I was doing some research for my upcoming first Hightower
Mystery novel which takes place on the Navajo and Hopi
Reservations, I came across my old manuscript.
And I thought why not now??

Marilyn
AUTHOR

CONTENTS

PREFACE

"Hope is the thing with feathers that perches in the soul - and sings the tunes without the words - and never stops at all."
   - Emily Dickinson

As they say, *"Hope springs eternal."* Another is that *"Soul is the fire within…"* But what if hope becomes shattered? What if the fire burns out? What do we have then? We have a *"Hollow Soul"*, something that reaches out for renewal, for filling up again. Sometimes we aren't able to do that before we need to.

This is a story about two people…a man and a woman…who meet, fall in love, but fight the 'game' of politics, and end up fighting for one another. Do they make it in time to save themselves? And their souls?

We can look for *"those feathers"* and HOPE and embrace it. We just need to do it quickly. I hope you enjoy this novel, revived from when I originally wrote it almost 30 years ago. And it still fits in to today's love stories, today's political climate, today's fears.

Marilyn
AUTHOR

CHAPTER 1

SOMEWHERE IN THE AIR, 1993

Hot, red flames roared up into the night sky, creating massive dark silhouettes that danced over the walls of the deep, cavernous kiva and the faces of the other Indians sitting around the fire. And then all eyes focused on one particular man, dressed in his full Kachina regalia, who swooped his immensely tall headgear toward the ground, then up toward the sky, raising his voice in loud, rhythmic majesty.

It wasn't that this man was a mix of white and Hopi Indian, instead it was a prophecy. A prophecy that would soon affect the entire continent called America. She watched him in wonder, thinking how grateful that she had met him, holding onto hope that he will be able to do what he must…for all of us.

She felt a bumping sensation and opened her eyes. She had been dreaming, remembering him from the time they had first met. She looked around the plane, feeling a bit groggy, wishing she had been able to stay in the dream.

Then she remembered where she was and what she was doing. How did this happen?

Here she was on a plane on route to the Southwest, with a fake name, alone and scared. *'Could she have done things differently? What did she do wrong? Should she have told him who she was before he got in so deep?'* Maybe then he would have had a different way out.

She felt the tears begin to fill her eyes. *'I can't lose control, not now. Not here. Not even when I get there. I need to be strong,'* she told herself.

What was her name again? She looked at her plane ticket, *'Eileen Raines'*. How long would she need to be this person? Forever? She was hiding, so most probably. She was no longer Maya Chardon, Anthropologist and occasional F.B.I. operative. She was no longer a woman who had seen more death and pain than she wanted to remember. *'Was there more death and pain ahead of her? Was she strong enough to handle that?'* She felt the tears again.

'Yes, I can do this. I have to do this, not just for me,' she thought. She suddenly felt a bit sick to her stomach. *'No, not now. Not here,'* she thought to herself. She really needed to settle down and find her strength. There was still hope. She just needed to find it.

She still had more than an hour left before they would land in Arizona. Then she would retrace her steps from the first time she was there, driving through the Navajo Reservation to the Hopi Reservation. It seemed so long ago when it had only been a few months.

'Will they still welcome her after all that has happened? Will they blame her? Will they blame him?' She had no other place to go. She had no other choice.

CHAPTER 2

THREE MONTHS EARLIER
THE WHITE HOUSE

The President of the United States rocked backward in his chair and attacked a paper clip, prying the curves out of it, trying to make it perfectly straight.

"So, what's going on, Pinky?"

The action with the paper clips was always a sign that he was going to rake someone over the coals. Today, it was to be the Director of the Central Intelligence Agency, Arthur Pinkerton.

"Which report would you like first, Mr. President?"

The President didn't look up but kept picking his fingernails with the paper clip and frowning slightly to himself. *"Last week's activity should be first, I think. Tell us the news and don't spend a week getting there, okay?"*

'Pinky' Pinkerton's stocky figure filled the chair and was still draped with his bulky trenchcoat. He felt very warm and nervous. His bald head was shiny with perspiration. Actually, he was sweating like a pig, which is really a poor metaphor – pigs don't sweat. He cleared his throat, picked up his notes, and began flapping his fat, loose lips in a monotone voice, *"The country of Peru has been engaged in an internal war between the countrymen and the Shining Path Senderistas since 1980, when that Marxist group set fire to the election ballots in the Andrean town of Chuschi. The Senderistas have become a torchbearer of world revolution. Across their country, small-town mayors, post-office employees, priests, police and even peasants who resisted them were gunned down. Over 25,000 lives have been lost and over 200,000 people have become refugees in their own country."*

The DCI stopped, and looking up to see the President watching him. Pinkerton felt relieved. He hadn't been sure the President had even been listening. He continued, *"The Upper Huallaga Valley is a source of much cocaine. Under the protection of the Shining Path, Columbian-piloted, light-plane traffic takes shipments from the Valley airstrips to Columbia for processing, and then on to the United States. Cocaine has brought between $20-$30 million a year to the Senderistas, funding their food, medicine and weapons to further their cause. The Bush Administration attempted negotiations with the government there for an effective anti-drug strategy, but the attempt failed because the rebels had overthrown the democratic government. The rebel movement has now spread, under the organized name 'Peru People's Movements' – staffed largely with Peruvian exiles in Germany, France, Sweden, Switzerland and Mexico."*

Once again, the DCI paused, this time to wipe his forehead with his soiled handkerchief. He returned the dirty fabric to his coat pocket, and adjusting his bulk in the inadequate chair, and continued, *"We became interested in assassinating the Shining Path leader, Abimael Guzman and learned of his plan to lead a raiding party in Bolivia, near the Peruvian border. Our strategy was for a full attack, wiping out the entire guerrilla group, which we did."* He looked up and nodded to a report on the President's desk, *"Unfortunately, Guzman was not with that particular group that day. All we really succeeded in doing was saving a Bolivian community from being massacred. We are formulating new plans, awaiting to hear from our well-placed informants."*

During Pinkerton's report, the Chief of Staff, Joel Wattenberg, was standing behind the President's desk, looking out the window. At the conclusion of the DCI's comments, he turned around abruptly, taking two steps forward with his hands clasped rigidly behind him. *"Yes, Pinkerton, you missed your target,"* he snapped. He sprang a step closer. *"And the press has been brutal."* Wattenberg leaned slightly forward, moving one hand to support himself on the edge of the President's desk,

"They are circling like buzzards, awaiting your next brilliant move." Satisfied he had achieved the effect he wanted, Wattenberg stood straight and again clasped his hands behind him, taking two steps backward.

The President appeared to ignore the comment, since he was looking for somewhere to place the blame for recent bad polls. His eyes focused on Pinkerton, *"Well, Pinky? Are you so sure now that you should have interfered in Peru last week?"*

"Actually, Mr. President, it was in Bolivia, against the Peruvian guerrillas. And yes, we should have made the attempt, just as we have done before in similar circumstances." He glanced at the chair beside him at the Chairman of the Joint Chiefs, who appeared shocked at the question, moving his well-manicured right hand upward to wipe a few beads of sweat from his bow. The DCI tried to hide his dislike for the President whenever they were in the same room, but he had no trouble letting his feelings be known to others. He suspected this latest verbal attack was the brainchild of Joel Wattenberg and managed a quick look at the younger man before adding, *"And, of course, as usual, you may recall we did consult you first and you agreed to the plan. Why are you concerned now?"*

The President nodded but did not speak. The Chairman of Joint Chiefs who had been quiet so far in this meeting, felt an urgency to fill the void, *"Yes, Mr. President, we all were included in that decision."*

The President nodded again but did not speak. Seconds passed and no one spoke.

The President of the United States, his jaw firm, his forehead a scowl, was again concentrating on his paper clip, sweat beads formed on his upper lip, a side bar of the exertion.

The President pinched the bridge of his nose, as if the stress of the day had delivered a migraine. He hoped that particular subject was now closed.

The President tightened, dropped his paper clip, and grabbed a computer printout, holding it aloft almost over his head, *"I am now at what I would call my lowest 'disapproval' rating ever. Because of last week's fiasco, this,"* he rattled papers over his head, *"reads 42 – down from 53. My opponents will be naming a Presidential candidate in a few short months, and I want this rating back up. This looks really bad for me."*

The DCI leaned towards the President, not an easy thing to do since his full girth was tightly squeezed into the chair, but he looked up at Wattenberg, *"Perhaps you could come up with an idea that will counteract the negatives of last week and help the President."* Pinkerton recognized Wattenberg as the real boss.

Wattenberg was once again by the window, and looked out, listening, but not responding. But he did nod smugly as if he believed Pinky and as if his approval meant everything. He needed a plan and would have one before the end of this meeting.

The President was making no effort to hide his anxiety, as he was now slouching in his chair, loosening his tie. For a moment he glared at the two men seated in front of his desk, but he couldn't keep his eyes from being drawn back to the sheaf of papers lying before him, back now on top of his desk.

"It's not as bad as it looks," his Chief of Staff said slowly, as he turned around and leaned back against the wall in his usual standing position, arms folded, trying to appear casual. There was a sense of tension in the air as this small group met in the Oval Office, attention drawn to the latest computer approval ratings. He smiled, saying to the group, but to no one in particular, *"There are three things to do now. Firstly,"* glancing toward Pinkerton, *"we simply forget last week ever happened. Secondly,"* now moving his eyes to a point somewhere above Pinkerton's head, *"we get as much good PR as possible out of the latest natural disasters."*

The President looked up at his Chief of Staff, *"How can we get good PR out of that when we assigned Corky to go out and see the victims?"*

Wattenberg has sent the frequently bewildered, youthful Vice President off on various assignments to keep him busy, and away from their strategy sessions, mainly because he felt the bumbling idiot flat out couldn't keep a secret. It was hardly believable that the *'ding-dong'* was just a heartbeat away from being the nation's commander in chief.

"Joel, sometimes I think you belong in a room made of thick sponge rubber." The two men seated before the President stared at him in astonishment as they watched their leader appear oblivious of them as he again pursued the slow, methodical cleaning of his fingernails with his straightened paper clip.

Even though the President occasionally treated him with a lack of respect, Wattenberg never showed his own intense personal dislike for the President. The man was his route, and he could bide the time it took to walk over him. Besides, the President only acted respectful outside of his circle of co-conspirators. With them, such crude words and actions were not new and were easily dismissible.

"You simply need to make some timely, well-publicized appearances at flood sites, like Chicago, several cities along the Mississippi, and tornado sites in Illinois, Kansas and Oklahoma. It should only take a couple of days. But most importantly, you can take with you additional Red Cross personnel and authorized people to hand out money for damages to qualified victims."

The President's eyes looked larger than life as he yelled at his Chief of Staff, banging his right fist on the desktop, scattering papers, *"Damn it, Joel, we don't have any money to give them anymore. Do you realize the number of floods and tornadoes we've had already this year?"*

"I know the exact number, but that is not important. We will find money, shifting some figures in the budget. Come up with a special new tax. Leave that to me."

The President's face wore an expression of disgust. *"Yeh, suckin' another buck from the taxpayer's tit,"* and made sucking noises. *"That'll really help my image."*

Wattenberg, used to such comments, ignored the President and continued, *"And, at the same time, we find out who the candidates will be for the opposition's party. They have no visible candidates out there making noises yet. But I can have the names within forty-eight hours."*

"Why?" asked the President stupidly, appearing to be absent-mindedly trying to return his newly straightened paper clip to its original curves.

Wattenberg frowned, as he knew it was too early to explain his ideas to his superior. He had more going on behind the scenes that were being carefully safe guarded. Soon it would be time to share his ingenious plan. But not here...not yet...not to the President nor his cronies. His frown smoothed out and the upper edges of his lips formed a slight smile.

"I can fill you in on that when we have the names, Mr. President."

"Whatever you say, Joel."

Wattenberg liked to hear that. He wanted the President to trust no one but him. He knew what to do. The best thing for the President would be an opposing candidate who was a Native American, so they could expose his selfish interests at the right time. The man he had in mind was Joseph Pahana – an increasingly popular man, the hero of the underdog. But the man is a symbolic amalgam of defined special interests centered around our government's unfortunate treatment of the American Indian. This whole idea was a scam – but a brilliant scam!

The President rocked forward in his chair now, still reworking the paper clip, almost oblivious of them. The meeting had dragged on long enough.

CHAPTER 3

A TELEVISION STUDIO

The distinguished attorney from Washington, D.C.., looked quite different without his Indian ceremonial garb. He was no longer communing with the Kachina spirits, but instead was dressed in a dark pin-stripe suit, about to appear on a television interview program. He had been asked on the show for two reasons: his celebrity popularity growing over the previous two years; and as a legal expert to follow up on an earlier program whose guest was the Chief Justice of the Supreme Court.

The attorney Joseph Pahana was absorbed in preparations by reviewing the previous program on videotape, where the host Damon Sloane was leaning forward with an intent look, quizzing the Justice, *"We've been talking a little about some of the most notable landmark cases the Supreme Court has made decisions on over the past few years, and there is something that puzzles me. Perhaps you can clear up the confusion for me. How can abortion be legal one decade and severely restricted the next? And why does the Supreme Court find capital punishment unconstitutional in 1972, yet four years later approve it? Does this show simply your conservatism, or is this supposedly a sign of your lack of guts, sir?"*

Joseph Pahana smiled to himself as he watched the tape. He didn't like Damon Sloane, few people did. The man looked like a modern-day hippie with his long hair and colorful clothes. And in Joseph's mind, Sloane was a *'sleeze-bag'*, who preyed on people's emotions when talking about logical issues. As a *'television journalist'*, sensationalism was his thing. And it worked, his show was one of the highest rated on TV. But he had to admit, the man was smart and did his homework.

Chief Justice Warren Paul Logan was a very dignified man in his 70's, with a shock of white hair that added a look of wisdom, when coupled with his black, bushy eyebrows and dark, imposing steel-cold eyes. Even though Sloane had just accused Logan's court of being *'wishy-washy'* in a sense, the elder statesman had shown no visible reaction, keeping his posture strong and straight, and his cold eyes glaring without flinching. He looked like a man afraid of no one and nothing. And Sloane was not about to succeed in his half-hearted attempt at intimidation.

"Many blame the shifts in decisions on the membership changes in the Court. These changes and political conditions do have their effect on Court decisions. But the highest impact is through the attorneys and their arguments before the Court. They should not stand on absolute rights, but be flexible in their demands, so that the Court has room to meet both the Court's needs and the interests of the litigating party. Judicial activism and original intention are both indispensable to the proper functioning of American constitutionalism. We are not an activist Court. We do not make the laws, we uphold them in the grand tradition of strict constructionists."

Sloane leaned a little more forward, as if he were anticipating a welcome battle, *"I read somewhere that you once said, 'Judgments made in the cold light of objective observation over a long and agonizing period of time are generally irrefutable.' But yet, you have been seen to change your own mind several times, even after you had publicly stated your judgment. And, because of this, several cases have taken many years before a decision was made by the Court."*

This seemed to bother the Chief Justice, especially since Sloane seemed to be attacking him personally. His eyes blinked several times, quicker than normal, and his expression reflected a concern he felt. But his voice didn't waver, as he responded strongly, *"There is a need to examine a case's impact in actual situations, seeing which constitutional provision and which principle of law should be applied and be determinant. Judgments need to be made on the Court's principles to cope with current problems and current needs. We need to be guided by the dual principles of original intention and current circumstances, with a greater emphasis usually on the latter."* Too late, the Chief Justice seemed to realize he had just repeated himself, and he felt slightly foolish.

There was an obvious leer on Sloane's face as he continued pushing, *"The Supreme Court has become embroiled in the political arena by issuing advisory opinions about the constitutionality of pending legislation, losing its judicial character while causing pileup and even more delay of legislation."*

Now the Justice realized where this was leading and appeared to steel himself for the battle, *"That is our job. The real original intention of the Founding Fathers was clearly to set up a system of 'mixed, balanced government,' that gave each branch a proper role and proportion of power, including the power to check one another. The legitimate needs of the judicial process outweigh the legislative branches. The Founding Fathers took great pains in creating and empowering the Supreme Court. They didn't want it to be tied to the same constituencies of other government branches for fear it wouldn't strike down acts of Congress and the President."*

"Tell me, Mr. Chief Justice, is that why your Court has been interfering lately in acts of Congress? Specifically, I would like to draw attention to the case of the Hopi Nation VS U.S.A."

If possible, it appeared that Justice Logan drew his posture even higher, *"In a word, Mr. Sloane, yes. For many Americans, famous, infamous and ordinary, the United States Supreme Court has been the last stop in their search for that elusive 'equal justice under the law.' The Court has the final word on all constitutional questions. That case did not belong on the floors of Congress for political debate in the first place. The case is a legal one, a 'petition for certiorari,' that our justice system must review."*

"And so you began review this past October, as one of the first cases argued in your Court?"

"That is correct."

"What did you think of the case?"

"The written argument, or brief, which was submitted by the Attorney of Record Mr. Joseph Pahana, is a superb legal piece. Rarely have I seen or heard a more complete brief. The legal historian who compiled this had the patience and imagination to perceive suspended or broken lines of legislative debate, knowing that somewhere there had to be buried additional records that formed contiguous data spelling out the missing pieces. If this all stands up, the conclusions would appear to be indisputable, supported by copies of the original, authentic papers."

Sloane turned toward the camera, "For those of you who may have been hiding on some deserted island, the case of the Hopi Nation VS U.S.A. has been called by the media, 'The most heinously insidious crime in the history of civilization.' The Hopi Indians, currently of Arizona, are accusing the white man's society of murder and genocide." Turning back to the Chief Justice, "The word is that these secret papers were in the archives of the Bureau of Indian Affairs all along. How did the Hopi Nation's representatives get a hold of them?"

Ignoring Sloane's question, the Chief Justice attempted a response, "There are actually several parts to this case, Mr. Sloane. You see, the Hopi people lay claim to being the First Americans having settled in the western hemisphere around 1140 AD. Anthropologists suggest these people were here as early as 700 AD. The Hopi Empire claims to be a sovereign nation. They say that the laws of the Constitution of the United States do not apply to their separate nation, and was made without their consent, knowledge or approval."

"But how can this be proven?"

"They have shown us photos of their sacred tablets, which are in the form of pictograms as they have no real written language. And, of course, there are copies of the treaties and supporting letters, which were thought to be missing (according to them) and were not even known to exist (according to our government). I cannot share all of the details with you, as there is a great deal of information that was provided to us. When the Court makes a decision on this case, the entire contents of the case will, of course, become a matter of public record."

"For just a moment, could we discuss the manner in which the documentation was obtained? There was an accusation, I believe, that the photos of the records were taken by a spy camera without authority. This being because they were in the sealed archives. Is that true?"

"If indeed the records were considered protected intelligence files, that would have meant unauthorized invasion of sealed government archives and would have been illegal. But sealed archives can be opened with warrants, which are available to any legitimate party with probable cause. There was nothing done illegally here."

"But wasn't there a part of the Court proceedings that was closed to the public, and why?"

"A portion was indeed not accessible to the public. We were investigating the origin of the documents. I shall anticipate your next question by telling you how we know they were authentic documents. In the days before copiers, when you couldn't simply flatten out aged or rotted parchment, or piece fragments together, and run a beam of light over the whole for an accurate facsimile, photographs, then later photostats, were made to be entered into the archives replacing the disintegrating originals. The watermarks on these archival photostats indicate a rare, steel filamentous paper designed to withstand the ravages of time and environmental conditions of the vaults. Thomas Edison invented it around the turn of the century, and it was ordered into limited archival use in 1910 or 1911. In those days, deficit spending, when it existed, was restricted to no more than several hundred-thousand dollars. The steel-threaded pages in these photos were enormously expensive – to convert thousands of historical documents into them would have broken the treasury. So, only a limited number were chosen, those documents determined by the government to remain beyond scrutiny for a minimum of 150 years. The watermarks on the photographs proved to the Court that without a doubt the evidence was authentic."

"Then, why was the case heard, and then a decision delayed?"

The Chief Justice's posture became less rigid, he breathed deeply and seemed to settle in his chair. *"There are many current-day concerns. In deciding this case, we need to consider its effect, based on the outcome. If the judgment is affirmative for the Hopi Nation, there are questions of real property rights as well as compensation questions. This case would be setting a precedent, which means the Court would need to provide guidelines for future 'like' cases. A great deal is involved. So further study and discussion within the Court is necessary before any further Court proceedings."*

"You sound as if you believe the Hopi Nation will win this case."

"Not at all. On the surface, the brief offers a seemingly accurate novelization of authentic history of what looks like documented origin. But any commentary on this case would be extremely premature. Our system of the rule of law in an open society requires expeditious adjudication of legal redress, the relief from injury as swift as possible and adequately compensatory. The decision in this case will be final and irrevocable. This case has the potential of not only changing our country's history but changing its future."

Sloane seemed to hesitate, realizing he was out of time, and began thanking the Chief Justice for appearing. Joseph Pahana stopped the tape. He had seen all he needed to see. He felt the Chief Justice had gone further than he had intended, which made the Justice look like a fool…and Joseph Pahana look like a hero. A slight smile played on his lips as he turned to take his position for his turn with Damon Sloane.

CHAPTER 4

A TELEVISION STUDIO

Joseph Pahana was a man of striking good looks – athletic build, a natural tan to his skin, dark-brown hair that was naturally wavy instead of straight, darker Indian hair. But it was his eyes that transformed him from an attractive man to a man of alarmingly good looks. His eyes seemed strong yet mystical, as if they were holding secrets, as if they could see deep within your mind.

He watched as Damon Sloane was being seated and wired across the table, speaking only when asked to recite something for a voice check for the audio levels. He had no respect for Sloane but was pleased to be on the program, as it would help his cause. He prepared himself mentally for Sloane's first question. He didn't really mind that Sloane introduced him as an attorney from Washington with a history of aiding the American Indian cause. It was true.

Sloane looked at Pahana for the first time when he asked, *"Tell me, Joseph Pahana, are you a religious man or a man interested in the world of politics?"*

Joseph felt surprised at the question and a frown knitted on his forehead as he attempted to answer, *"I'm not sure what you mean by that question, but I suppose that I would have to say both."* He would have to be careful not to appear defensive in the way he phrased his answers. He learned an immediate lesson, never to underestimate Damon Sloane.

"Let's talk religion first. You are both Hopi Indian and white. Which part are you feeling right now?"

"If the question is which religion do I honor, I am Hopi in

my beliefs. That is my culture. It means that I firmly believe in peaceful solutions to problems."

"Are you saying we all need to find religion in order to find peace?"

"Find religion? Many think of religion as going to church on Sundays, singing hymns and tithing. In that sense, no. It would change nothing." He looked into the camera, *"Religion should mean individual spirit – how we think and feel about ourselves and all that we care about. The healing begins within each of us. Once healing has begun, then we will begin to smile again and actually feel at peace within ourselves. And each of us will demand changes that affect us. We will no longer accept nor be satisfied with either venal or stupid actions by others, in our families, in our business world, and in our government. And this will affect the way we treat one another not just within our own country, but with other countries. We can only respect others' rights to their own actions and decisions once we respect ourselves and our country."*

"Whoa. Are you saying that if we learn to respect ourselves, we will find peace?"

"That is one of the ways, yes."

"All right, so you practice the Hopi religion. Does that means you don't respect the Bible?"

Damn, Joseph didn't like the way this was going. Religion wasn't why he was here. Justice was. Perhaps he could turn the discussion in the right direction soon. *"The Bible is the Holy Book of Judaism and Christianity, the most widely known book in the English-speaking world. I respect and have indeed read the Bible, Mr. Sloane."*

"If you an Indian, why read the Bible?"

"The Bible is essential for understanding many of the moral

and spiritual values of our culture, whatever our religious beliefs. The story of Abraham and Isaac concerns our deepest feelings about the relations between parents and children. The story of Job is a major representation in our tradition of being patient during suffering. The Parables and sayings of Jesus, such as 'Blessed are the meek for they shall inherit the earth,' are so often alluded to that they need to be known by Americans of all faiths." Pahana leaned forward for emphasis, "But, what the Bible says has been interpreted so many ways that we have to acknowledge that we each choose an interpretation – whatever suits our needs and makes sense for us."*

He continued, *"All educated speakers of American English need to understand what is meant when someone describes a contest as being between David and Goliath, or whether a person who has the 'wisdom of Solomon' is wise or foolish, or whether saying 'My cup runneth over' means the person feels fortunate or unfortunate. Those who cannot use or understand such allusions cannot fully participate in literate English."*

Then, Pahana sat back in his chair smiling, *"The linguistic and cultural importance of the Bible is a fact that no one denies. No person in the modern world can be considered educated without a basic knowledge of all the great religions of the world – Islam, Confucianism, Taoism, Buddhism, Judaism, and Christianity.*

"That should take care of the religious issues, Mr. Sloane. Now why don't we talk about the real reason I'm here?" He folded his hands in a steeple in front of his chin, resting his elbows on the arms of the chair, looking very reverent, almost holy, untouchable.

"All right. Let's talk about the state of our world, our country, and politics. Why don't you tell us how you think we're doing, Mr. Pahana?"

"I am sad to say that the state of our world is bad. The wonderful concept of the sociability of nations has been one the

people in this country have always wanted. Instead, we seem to continually be antagonistic, with a high degree of belligerence exercised by all nations against one another at all times. Does this perhaps return to a core of interference? Is a nation such as the United States so full of itself, feeling so bloated with egotism that we must continually interfere with other nations in their acts of building their economies and class distinctions? At times, the U.S. acts like a dictator, in our attempts to force our ideals on others. Every empire throughout history had to get to the point where it loses its swelled head. No one country should dominate – that is what causes war. This country should take care of its own business – which we are having trouble doing. The age of dominance must end and an age of cooperation must begin."

"How would you change things, Mr. Pahana?"

"Well, our main problem has been a lapse of initiative towards a common goal of peace. When people don't agree actively on an objective, there's much less dynamic effort," and then he smiled, *"and that actually makes life a lot less interesting."* Returning to a serious look again, *"Perhaps we have lost our true goals – once we start rationalizing and cutting corners, we'd better watch out, because we may be fooling ourselves and others with the 'nobility' of our goals as we now recognize them. What is wrong with starting over again? Of creating a new political system that would work for us today, still based on an autocratic government? What an exhilarating idea! Otherwise, are we simply recreating our ignorance? And who could lead us through this redesign? Today, the main activity that draws men of talent seems to be business. But our world of business will not stand if our government fails. And the 90's recession is telling us that. 'Public business' should command their allegiance and their time. But you see, they are paid so handsomely, that they would need to take great pay cuts – what a paradox! These formidable leaders with extraordinary qualities of leadership could help us solve our overriding moral dilemmas.*

"*The U.S. public as a whole is not concerned with solving the problems of the poor, of the homeless. But they should be, because these ultimately will be dangerous to everyone's 'ordinary life'. We are witnessing the disappearance of the positive goal. We've never stopped to sufficiently contemplate the advantages or disadvantages of modern nationalism. And there is more – the loss of 'moral sense,' of knowing the difference between right and wrong, and of being governed by it. Our lost moral sense includes the rise of all of these: corruption in government; corruption in the world of business; crime on our streets and in our homes; sexual immorality; loss of family unity; increased drug dependency; lack of value for life itself; and lastly, we won't listen, as we proceed to ruin our environment, our air and water, our natural world itself. Let us hope and pray that there is nothing permanent about things the way they are right now. None of this is news to any of us. We read it every day in the papers, we pay for it with our taxes, and we pay for it with our lives.*"

Sloane looked warm, his forehead and top lip showed sweat, as the interview continued, "*But isn't the government still the one to turn to?*"

Pahana leaned back in his chair, looking down at his hands, now relaxed in his lap, and shook his head slowly, sadly, "*No.*" Then, as he looked up, first at the camera, and then at Sloane, he told us why, "*The government cannot be our friend – it is just an instrument. Where should we look for answers? We should look in the mirror. Each one of us needs to reexamine our own sense of values and morals. And, we should then apply this higher, renewed sense of caring to everything that concerns our lives.*"

"*Is that why you have turned to the Supreme Court instead of the legislature, Mr. Pahana, to get what you and your people want? You have appealed with your so-called brilliantly evolved brief directly to the Supreme Court, turning your back on this country, representing a small nation of Indians. Where are your values and morals, Mr. Pahana?"*

At last, here was the issue at hand. *"I am an attorney, Mr. Sloane. I have many clients, some individuals, some corporations, some groups. I have had occasion to represent several American Indian Nations in legal circumstance. In the Supreme Court this past October, yes, I presented a legal argument for the case of the Hopi Nation VS U.S.A. Actually, in legal terms it's not an appeal. No decision was made in a court of law that requires overturning, like in appellate procedures, and it WAS upheld in Court at least once. But it IS an appeal in the broader sense – an appeal to right a wrong. I am not at liberty to discuss this case more, since it is still active and pending. However, I can speak about such cases in the general sense.*

"There have been many cases of criminal injustice before this country's judicial system. Recidivism is a term the criminal courts have lived with for years. This case, and many cases before, especially with the American Indians, use the term 'genocide'. The dictionary defines this term as 'the systematic, planned annihilation of a racial, political, or cultural group'. Such activity by the white man to the American Indian has been documented in laws, treaties, authentic letters of the time, history books, literature, television, and even in the movies. It is not shocking new news. However, there are accounts of real events, which bring the picture of this deed home to us.

"All Indian tribes have been hunted like animals and massacred by the thousands. What a great motif of westward expansion. A nation of white men – whose existence and growth were predicated upon the primary sanctity of property rights. This country's history has a shadow of death of a race, the tragedy of a continent – for greed."

For a few seconds there was numb silence. Joseph Pahana's eyes were dark and angry. The camera moved to concentrate on Damon Sloane's face, waiting for his next comment. He appeared lost in a daze, staring at Joseph Pahana, until he noticed someone signaling to him. Appearing somewhat more composed, he said, *"Umm, yes, all of that sounds horrible and cruel. But it was so long ago. That isn't happening today."*

Joseph's eyes were glaring at Sloane, *"Oh yes, it still continues today. It's only the methods that have changed. Greed is an unholy business partner. In the moral sense, many Indian tribes still retain what is generally termed 'aboriginal rights' to at least a portion of the lands they have occupied for thousands of generations. But they are slowly starving, dying from disease and exposure, from lack of medical attention, and infant mortality, and being poisoned by contaminated water. Much of their land has been designated as National Sacrifice Areas. The Department of Defense and the former Atomic Energy Commission have declared the Black Hills of South Dakota so heavily contaminated that they should become a national nuclear waste dump. The Indians there have a spiraling rate of cancer and birth defects. The Indian people are being sacrificed as if they were lab rats in some huge scientific experiment, their lives considered expendable."*

"And so you have taken several cases to the Supreme Court for help. Do you think they can help your people, I mean, your clients?"

"The Supreme Court has become so deferential to the elected branches of government that constitutional rights are less likely to be judiciously enforced than ever before. Today's conservative Court feels that democracy means majority rule rather than right VS wrong; that legislatures and executives, because they are elected, are majoritarian; and that the courts are not elected and therefore not majoritarian. Therefore, the courts should only overturn elected branches of government if a clear constitutional principle exists and is not being served by the electorate. But the very existence of a constitution is counter-majoritarian. The Court's approach to judicial review with a majoritarian rule is anti-constitutional. Fewer and fewer constitutional clauses are being enforced. The government

prevailed in 82% of the non-unanimous decisions in constitutional cases that came before the Court in the last five years. By contrast, a little over 20 years ago, the government prevailed in only 25% of the constitutional decisions. Without judicial enforcement, the constitution is little more than the parchment that sits under glass in the National Archives."

"I understand that religion is a main focus of an Indian culture. Do you, as an Indian, practice and support spiritual healings? Sometimes it can actually keep someone from being saved, as in the case of the son of David and Ginger Twitchell, the Christian Scientists."

"Spiritual healing has existed for several thousands of years and has been part of many religious beliefs. It is legally so today, in many states. No one should be penalized for their religious beliefs, no matter what cost they have to pay."

Sloane frowned, *"Are you condoning murder through reckless disregard?"*

"The white man has murdered more people than the American Indians have. You are a white man, you answer that question."

Sloane sat back in his chair, wiping his forehead and relaxing for a moment. Putting his hand over his mouth, he seemed to study Joseph Pahana for a moment more before saying, *"You take on such cases against all odds, are you a modern-day hero?"*

Joseph Pahana began to laugh, deeply and fully, *"Am I a hero? That feels weird, because public opinion of heroes generally means Superman and Elvis. Many heroes we never even hear of. In my mind, a hero is one that cares about others and does something to help. A hero is one who values life by actively saving* others' lives. You see what I mean? Wouldn't it be wonderful to have a hero for President? Again? Yes, we had a President, his name was George Washington, who was a true hero. He was a remarkable man in every aspect of his character, in his courage, in his persistence, and in his amazing belief that he was right, and that he would prevail in spite of enormous frustrations and difficulties."

A look of interest came over Sloane's face, *"You still didn't answer my question of your being a hero. He was a hero, are you comparing yourself to him?"*

This time Pahana simply chuckled, *"No, I don't compare myself to him – not at all. Except that I believe in my own inner convictions. It doesn't mean that I am perfect, because I am human and humans are imperfect. I do believe in the same basic things George Washington did. He had faith – in providence."*

"Faith in providence. Does that mean he believed in God?

This brought a smile and another chuckle. *"So many have said they appealed to God for help and guidance in the Presidency. For example, Ronald Reagan, Jimmy Carter, Gerald Ford, Richard Nixon, L.B. Johnson. But that's phrase-making. The question is whether they had the confidence or faith that they were doing the right thing. That's what providence is – doing the right thing. By whose rules? That is where the Creator enters the picture."*

Sloane's next question seemed obvious, *"Are you preparing to run for President?"*

It was hard to read Joseph Pahana's face, as he answered, *"I have not thought much along those lines. I only recognize what my goal is – to help others reestablish their moral bearings, to become caring and honest. I have been touring and speaking, not to teach ethics. You don't learn that from sermons and preachers. I don't pretend to have that power over others. I am only here to remind people that they have slipped. They have forgotten. It is time to remember, before we destroy ourselves and our world."*

"What qualifies someone, do you think, to run for President in our country, Mr. Pahana?"

With a mocking smile, he answered, *"The ability to get elected."*

As the music came up in the background, Sloane looked almost sad as he said, *"We've run out of time. Will you come back? I think we've only just begun to talk."*

"I will always be happy to sit and talk with you, Damon. Anytime." He looked from Sloane into the camera with a big smile.

CHAPTER 5

THE WHITE HOUSE

The President was feeling anxious, as he waited as usual, for the rest of his so-called comrades to meet him in the Situation Room, buried in the lowest levels of the White House.

They came racing in from the steel-gray corridors of the underground complex of the White House, looking physically rumpled of clothes, but more importantly, rumpled of countenance.

The large round table in the Situation Room had been highly polished, reflecting in the indirect lighting, the somber faces of the bodies seated around it.

Joel Wattenberg, who had ushered everyone in, closed the door, glancing at the table to make sure everyone had a copy of his interview plan, and proceeded to begin pacing, speaking as if he were dictating, very much in charge. *"I assume you've all seen the newspaper."* To illustrate which paper and which article he meant, he reached into his dropped briefcase and pulled one out, reading the headlines aloud, *"'Hero of the people running for President?' And I'd like to quote just a few comments from this story, 'In an interview on last evening's Damon Sloane Show, Washington D.C. attorney Joseph Pahana showed, once again, how cool he can remain under pressure, how he can commentarily rip apart the government, from the legislature to the Supreme Court, all while retaining his winning smile. He is believable. He is constructive in his criticism. He makes it all seem possible. And when asked if he may be in the running for the nation's highest office, he didn't necessarily say no.' This is a man who on the surface may seem like the most popular candidate to run against our President."*

The President was the first to comment, *"Sure an American Indian who had the temerity to learn to read English and suggested to his Indian superiors who themselves could barely read English, that certain restrictions placed on the reservations of their Hopi Nation were too severe."*

DCI Pinkerton quickly leaned forward to add, *"Several of the Court's judges admitted crying their eyes out when they read his case – the whole litany of deceit and dishonesty, killing and starving entire tribes, original settlers of this country. What they did and how they did it – the so-called cruelty of the white man. I really think it was the way the brief played up the Spaniards and the French and how they loved the Indians. It made us look all that much worse."*

The Director of the F.B.I. Gavin Patrick Lafferty O'Toole felt his face redden, making quite a contrast with his partially gray hair, bespeaking a once full crown of bright red. He felt himself vying for attention as he spoke in an almost-too-loud voice, *"That Hopi case is pretty damned scary, if you ask me. Not just because of the obvious payment in land and monies we would have to turn over, but the fact that it is so strongly based on a staggering premise, an earth-shaking concept – a magnificent obsession, showing how vulnerable the powers that be in our federal government are. And, even worse, those Indians could win. Several members of the Court have expressed how strongly they feel that the Hopi case may be built on a firm foundation of constitutional law. Of course, they haven't yet rendered their final decision."*

The President didn't like the sound of that, turning to look at his Chief of Staff, *"Joel, do they have a chance of winning, do they have proof of what they say?"*

Wattenberg took a deep breath and looked away, apparently the President hadn't read the papers, *"The case appears to be solid, at least on paper. The U.S. government stole the lands of the Hopi through a series of conspiracies in which promises were spelled out in treaties, treaties that were ignored by the government as if they weren't worth the paper written on. These papers were then buried in the sealed archives of the Bureau of Indian Affairs in Washington. Some treaties were considered part of the record, others were buried in the vaults. Historical real estate was supposedly compensated by the coin-of-the-era, as spelled out by the Supreme Court in 1912 or 1913…"*

Unnoticed the Vice President was sitting at the table, just waiting his chance at comment. He decided to interrupt, since what Joel was saying seemed boring. He tried to appear casual, folding his hands behind his head, stretching, saying, *"Those judicial fruitcakes wouldn't dare give them back the land – they would never survive the polls."*

Surprisingly, no one laughed, at least out loud, but the President, slightly irritated, managed to treat his young friend with patience, *"Corky, I don't think they have to, but I see what you mean. Unfortunately, if these Indian servers of renewed briefs and demands succeed in getting Supreme Court support and approval, our own popularity is nix. Because our white-man constituency won't like losing their land, homes and rights. It's like whose rights come first here? We've got to come up with something to stonewall or kill the issue. Unless we can find someone else to blame. Certainly can't blame this one on Mother Nature."*

Joel Wattenberg recognized his opening, *"Unlike the flooding, tornadoes and the new disease we seem to have developed this year, you're right. Mother Nature had nothing to do with this one. However, we can take advantage of it, and ultimately get rid of this Indian and his causes."* All attention focused on this brilliant young man. No one in the room liked him, but they had respect for his mind. He was a boy wonder who only a few years earlier had rescued a failing campaign and placed his boss in the White House. He was also a manipulator who had clawed his way through the inner circle until he was second in command. He had the President's ear and that was all that mattered to him. All else would follow.

"From all of our information, there are two men who stand out as viable candidates. One is from the South, Senator Clarence Edward Bowles, Harvard man, married to a doctor who looks like a female rendition of Ichabod Crane. So they are very high in the social circles, in both politics and medicine. We could dig up dirt on them, no problem, if needed. And of course, Joseph Pahana is the other potential candidate that our opponents are considering. I understand he has been consulting with various members of the party already." Wattenberg paused, looking at the F.B.I. Director, *"How does he check out, O'Toole?"*

"Clean as a whistle, except for his involvement with this dirty Indian business. He doesn't drink or womanize. Hell, I think the guy's still a virgin. We haven't found any woman in his life, even back in college. No man either, in case you wondered. Maybe there's something in his beliefs that he has to save himself for marriage."

There was light laughter around the table. *"So sorry, Joel, the guy is so Clorox, he makes the sheets squeak. He's a Goddamn boy scout!"*

Pinky had to add his two cents, *"They say he's a tribal god, an icon who can control the future of this world, for Christ's sake! I don't believe such a being exists, and certainly not one that we've educated in our much-hated-by-them white man's schools."*

"I don't care if you believe it or not, and it doesn't really matter whether we believe it, does it?" Wattenberg smiled to himself as he looked at the men and women around the table, part of the President's legion. They are some of the most important leaders in the country, and they are like women in combat – weak and led by emotion. What a wonderful tragedy. Wonderful because he's the only real leader here. He leaned over the table, giving them his leadership stare, *"We're talking about a conspiracy*

here. A conspiracy mounted by the enemies of democracy to bring the honorable giant to its knees and destroy our beloved America's first-strike capabilities worldwide. We have a nation to think about – and ourselves. We'd look like damned fools if we let this 'god' win the job that rules our nation. But we can use him – literally even publicly support the notion of a minority as President. We watch our opponents nominate him at their convention and begin their campaign. Then we strike – abusing his name and watch him fall. Watch that whole party fall as they scramble last minute for a new candidate without time enough to successfully promote him into the elections. I have a plan that will work! Hell, it's ingenious!"

The President appeared mesmerized by his Chief of Staff. He nodded with his customary approval of Joel's suggestions. He allowed Joel to sweat the details, never having been a real detail man himself.

"But how? What kind of plan do we have?" Pinky was anxious to know, especially since it may involve something illegal. He would love a chance to nail this son-of-a-bitch. With Wattenberg gone, maybe he and the others would have some influence over the President.

"It's really very simple. And very legal, Pinky." The DCI's body language betraying him, hating his now-slumping bulk that reflected his disappointment. Wattenberg stood straight, arms rigidly clenched behind him, as he dictated his new plan. *"What we have here is a very un-American man, embattled in a war between the Executive and the Judicial. If there's a grain of validity in that brief, we'd all be prosecuted under the laws of Congress for covering up something that we had absolutely nothing to do with over a hundred years ago for the sake of political advantage. Everybody loses. We recognize that the cost is beyond the extra-ordinary.*

"So, gentlemen, this is the way the game shall be played. The Supreme Court is like an unseen, unelected government

behind the government. The Supreme Court's docket holds many cases from child pornography to antitrust. Granted the brief Joseph Pahana submitted is considered one of the most brilliant ever received by the judiciary, a model of legal analysis. But who says the Court has to make a decision on the Indian case before the election? We need to stonewall to delay the issue more. As we have successfully done before, we could begin some well-placed anti-abortion activities, or use some other issue before the Court to stonewall. Lobbyists can be made use of. The Court would have to table the Indian cause because this brief is newer, and they need to follow the dated agenda. And let us keep in mind, that there are other Indian issues out there either enroute to, or already before the Supreme Court, the summaries of which would provide a pile of papers several inches thick.

"Shortly before the election, at the perfect time, we let slip a rumor – a so-called Pahana plan. You see, we have at least three Supreme Court justices who are practically on their deathbeds, and who won't be around shortly after next year's elections. The 'new' President would find himself in the position of appointing a new Secretary of the Interior, and several new justices, who would be, naturally, sympathetic to the President's causes. So, this rumor is that Pahana planned arranged deaths for three of the justices, planning to blame them on the late justices' health, or if the deaths come under suspect, which they would, blame would move to the Aryans or Nazis or the Klan, some identifiable collection of domestic terrorists, some radical band of vigilantes. The motive wouldn't be hatred or rage – but Pahana's manipulation, to replace those justices with new ones sympathetic to the Indian cause. The rumors would grow in strength, and the party would have to rid itself of a tainted candidate. And, if they are stupid enough to keep him on as candidate, it would cost Pahana a great deal of support. And, of course, we all know that their party, in reality, is so naïve that they couldn't think that far ahead. Joseph Pahana becomes the bad guy in the history books. If I recall, he did say something recently about Indians not being portrayed properly in the history books.

Well, we would certainly take care of that, wouldn't we?"

The others at the table seemed to take a moment to consider Wattenberg's plan. The only female in the room, who was generally ignored, was the first one to see the larger picture. Attorney General Pegi Levin-Gallagher seemed thoughtful as she spoke, *"So, you're saying, Joel, that Joseph Pahana would be placed in an awkward position of having to defend himself, which would make him only look guiltier."* There was a murmur of approval about her thought, as she continued, staring at Wattenberg, *"And, after our reelection, we could take advantage ourselves of any deaths on the Court – natural deaths, of course."* Everyone smiled at that. *"And we could push in our own replacements, who just happened to hate Indians, and will either kill their case or dismiss it. Then we're back in the slue, and the country's safe. Right?"*

Wattenberg liked the Attorney General – she was tough and fierce at her job, and never said anything until she was ready – and it was always to the point. *"Exactly, Pegi."*

"Well, congratulations, Joel," she admired his brilliant mind too. *"Indians give me the creeps. It's like they know something we don't. I support your plan."*

O'Toole of the F.B.I. felt his face redden, he hated both of them. They were heartless in everything they did. Two peas in a pod. *"Well, Pegi, I must say. That really says it all. Very profound."*

The room emptied within seconds, except for Wattenberg and the President, who turned to his Chief of Staff with a question, *"Wouldn't it be a good idea to get someone inside Pahana's group? So we can keep track of him?"*

Joel found himself disturbed and angered by O'Toole's remarks and had to force himself to pay attention. *"I agree. What do those F.B.I. yo-yos know, anyhow? We'll let them bring in that girl of theirs on this – the one who loves the Indians? She'll probably only report the good things to us, so we can feed that to their party and solidify his nomination. And, in the meantime, we'll assign some special agents for our side to follow him and deal with any problems. For the girl's benefit, we can call the assignment…'a mission of compassionate inquiry'."*

The President laughed, *"Damn, Joel, you're good at what you do. You're my own personal leopard. Mean. Meat-eating. Never changing. The leopard has spots when he's born and he has spots when he dies. You are definitely a leopard."*

Wattenberg made a type of growl and practiced a leopard-type smile. But it looked more like the Cheshire Cat.

CHAPTER 6

IN THE RAINFOREST

Maybe she shouldn't have come. It was so hot, and she felt so alone. She looked at the unopened envelope in her hands, a message from the outside world. But she wasn't quite ready to open it yet.

She was in a small rustic village near the rainforest where she had just buried her father. She looked around her, seeing the shabby hotel room, the broken mirror that made her reflected face look like a Picasso-style jagged painting. And she felt the heat, oh how she felt the heat. 102 degrees outside, at least 110 degrees inside, what felt like 100% humidity, no air conditioning, broken ceiling fan, cold-and-cold running water. The air hung like a cape over this valley; she missed the cooler, more forgiving air of Boston. She could feel the bed's broken coils under her hot, tired back as she closed her eyes and tried to picture her father's face.

She saw his dark hair, unkempt as usual, his heavy-browed, dark eyes, the perfect nose and teeth. And his smile. Tears burned her eyes as she remembered how she loved his smile. And it had always been directed towards her, his beautiful, genius daughter. And oh, how she had always adored him, her frequently-absent, but dedicated father.

She had attended her father's alma mater, taking the same courses in Anthropology, the study of humanity, physical and cultural characteristics, social relationships, etc. She even had followed his specialty into Cultural Anthropology. But, unlike her father's interest in the Mayan civilization, she had always been fascinated with Native Americans, in trying to uncover underlying patterns and structures of their languages, mythologies, gender roles, symbols and rituals. Still, she followed his footsteps again as the Curator for the Pre-Columbian Collection at the Peabody Museum at Harvard University.

All of this had been theirs to share, just between father and daughter. Even her husband and son had been shared, in a way. Her father had introduced her to the man she grew to love, and their son had looked so much like his grandfather; at least, by the age of three he had.

Now they were all just memories, the men she had loved and lost. Only her pain and loneliness were hers alone.

Coming back here was affecting her more than she had anticipated. She found herself lonely and depressed. And so damned hot!

She had to get outside. Maybe she could breathe out there. The streets were dusty, covering everything with a thin layer. She could even taste it in the air. Such an ancient, squalid town. So much like it had been for hundreds of years, except today it offered off-and-on running water and electricity in its hotel.

The villagers here smiled all the time. That was one of the things that fascinated her so much, the simplicity of their lives that were so charged with happiness. They worked all day long, seven days a week, yet cared so much for life and one another. The simpler cultures here were like that of the Native Americans. She envied them. Maybe her father had, too. Envied them their simple, but seemingly full, peaceful lives. The world outside this place had made living so complicated, almost too complicated to bear. She felt so sad, yet here she could find a peacefulness not available 'back home'. A large part of her didn't want to leave this town.

She remembered her first visit here to this Mayan village, one of the few that still honored their tradition, still speaking the old language.

It was years ago. And she had asked her father, *"What is it about these people that intrigues you so much?"*

He had laughed, turning towards her, sweeping his arms in the air around them, *"Don't you feel it? The history, my dear daughter. Feel the history. The Mayans who lived here so long ago were alarmingly intelligent – so much more appealing than their Aztec and Inca contemporaries. They were more mysterious and their way of life so much more paradoxical."*

He grew excited, talking about his life's study, *"Just think of it, these people were technologically a stone-age people, knowing nothing of metal tools or weapons, or even wheel and plow. Yet, they reached a high level of intellectual and aesthetic sophistication. By AD 600 – so long ago – these social agriculturists had conquered arithmetic, astronomy, and calendric development. They developed a form of writing and a broad, practical knowledge of medicine."*

Still sweeping his arms about, *"We are standing in the middle of their empire, which stretched throughout the Yucatan Peninsula and adjacent areas of Mexico and Guatemala. There is a riddle here – and I must solve it. The reasons for their rise, their accomplishments, the causes for their decline. For centuries archaeologists and scholars like myself have been trying to figure it out, trying to reconstruct Mayan life.*

"I find it hard to understand why you don't share my feelings. You're my daughter. It should be there in your blood. Why don't you join me here in my study and help me solve these riddles? We could be a team."

She had put her arms around her father, *"You are amazing. Yes, it is all in my blood, this need to search for ancient truths. But there is more in my blood, Dad. Yours too. I want to study our own heritage, our American Indian heritage. We have a history out there too. Our ancestor Bolivar, son of Francois Chardon and his Indian wife, Ychon-su-mous-ka, Sand Bar. You*

were named for him. Listen to your name, Francois Bolivar
Chardon."

And he had laughed at her, *"Listen to your own name.
Maya, named for these people right here."*

He saw how serious she felt about this. *"Okay, continue
your ancestral story.."*

*"I only know a little of their story. Francois worked for the
American Fur Company, as trader and interpreter. In the 1830s,
he met and became friends with artist-author George Catlin. I've
read about them. Catlin even saved our ancestor's life once, kept
him from being trampled by a buffalo. They spent years together,
getting to know the Crow and Mandan Indians. Look at me, Dad. I
look like her – Sand Bar. George Catlin painted her picture, I saw
it in his book. She was beautiful, richly dressed, the upper part of
her dress all covered with brass buttons. Her hair was dark, soft
and glossy like silk, falling over her shoulders in waves produced
by the braids that Indian women wore then. Catlin even talked
about how Bolivar, their only child, was raised by relatives in
Philadelphia."*

He had said he understood her interest, but his eyes had
reflected a sadness. How she wished she could reach out and hug
him now. Her sad heart and thoughts were full of memories as she
stopped at the edge of the town, looking toward the mountains
and rainforests he had shown her. He had wanted to share the
wonders with her, even taking her to the deserted jungle center of
Bonampak, where the wall paintings showed scenes of Mayan life.

Her father had known he would die here someday. In this
tropical rainforest in Northern Guatemala; and so he had selected
a phrase from one of the three great Maya classics from highland
Guatemala for her to recite at his burial. The Rabinal-Achi, Act IV,
from the dance-drama, virtually the only Mayan one in existence:

"Kiss your mountains goodbye

And your valleys
Because you're going to die in this place
To disappear in this place.
We'll cut your vine here – your trunk
We'll cut your lineage here
Here under sky
Here on the earth."

Yesterday, in his death ceremony near this small Mayan village, she had recited this verse for him. Now she must leave this place, saying goodbye to her father for the last time. She must continue to pursue her own dreams, to solve her own riddles.

Back in the privacy of her room, she looked at the envelope she held, addressed to Maya Chardon. Years before, she had tried to explain to her husband why she wouldn't be accepting his name, that she was proud of her heritage and it wouldn't be right for a French-Indian to have an Italian last name. He never understood. It didn't matter now. She had only one other name, and it was on the sheet inside the envelope. At once, it made her forget her pain and the heat. It said,

> *"Pumpkin...we need you back home. Ticket*
> *waiting at airport. Meet you on return this*
> *Friday...E.T."*

Elliott Tanner. She hadn't heard from him in almost two years. It seemed strange to see her code name again on paper. When she had 'quietly' joined the Federal Bureau of Investigation after college, they had selected 'Pumpkin' from the Seneca Indian tribe sacred curing songs from the Society of the Mystic Animals. To her it had sounded more like a term of endearment than a code name. This had been the only secret that she had kept from her father. Her father was her best friend. But he wouldn't have understood she could be a buffer for the Indians with the government, as they fought for their rights. Sometimes she did help, but sometimes, in her intelligence assignments, she was afraid she only gave the government information ammunition to hurt the Indians.

"Why did the Bureau need her now?" Well, why not? At least they had waited until after her father's death ceremony. And maybe it would take her mind off her painful memories.

She would welcome anything to displace the hurt she was feeling. And the timing was convenient, she had just started a short sabbatical from her work, mainly to deal with her father's death. She was at a crossroads – facing her past and trying to find her future.

As she packed, she laughed out loud, *"I feel like a God-damn Superman…by day an anthropologist at a museum; by night an F.B.I. agent."* She was starting to feel a little better

CHAPTER 7

LOGAN AIRPORT

Tanner was at the airport, waiting just as he said he would be, except he had a bouquet of flowers in his arms. Maya couldn't help but smile at his effort to conceal the real reason he was there from anyone who might see them. The last time he had brought her flowers was before her wedding, when he asked her not to get married. She still didn't know if that was because he cared for her, or that he feared the Bureau would be losing her. Maybe it was a little of both.

She decided to surprise him and flew into his arms as if he were her long-lost lover and gave him a passionate kiss. His face turned red and sweat began to bead his lower lip. She was right, he cared. But she could never feel more than respect for her sporadic superior – not even friendship. She had seen how stern and cold-hearted his business had made him.

He had a car waiting. They exchanged small talk until they arrived at her home in Belmont, a suburb of Boston. This was the house she had completely redecorated after her husband and son died. She just couldn't bring herself to sell it. Perhaps it was the one thing that she could cling to with her memories that represented the days when she felt so completely happy. She found she could tolerate the house. Besides, it was the only home she had now.

Then, why didn't it feel like 'home' when they entered? As they settled into overstuffed chairs in the living room, the only feeling she found here in this house was 'familiar'. Well, that was something at least.

"So, Elliott, why don't you tell me what this is all about."

"Maya, you have always been the best operative we have
had in your specialty. Whenever we have had problems with the
Native Americans, you were there for us. You would do a job
quickly and cleanly for us. Now, we need you like we never have
before."

Tanner leaned over and took out a dossier from his case.
Pulling a picture from the file, he handed it to her, "Do you
recognize this man?"

She looked at a slightly familiar face she had seen in the
news many times. "Yes, it's Joseph Pahana." Looking up at
Tanner, she kept on with her explanation. "He is a mix of Hopi
Indian and white. Born 1960, lived on the reservation in Arizona
until his teens. He attended BIA (Bureau of Indian Affairs High
School) in Phoenix. When his father died, he went on to college. I
believe he graduated from Harvard Law School cum laude. He
moved to Washington, D.C., and has represented American
Indians in various dealings since. He also tours and speaks
around the country, talking about saving our souls and saving the
planet." She studied the picture closer, smiling at herself. She had
heard he was supposed to be quite charismatic.

Tanner took the picture back, looking at it. "Yes, he
retained his Indian name Pahana, because he has been
recognized by his people as their 'savior' whom they have always
been waiting for. For the past ten years, we have had him tagged
as a religious and legal Indian fanatic. Now, we think something
else is happening. We think he may be considering a political
career. And not just ANY career – THE career – running for
President."

"But Elliott, that would be against his religion. At least, I
think it would. Generally, the Hopi people have a policy of non-
involvement. But maybe that changes with the appearance of their
'savior' called Pahana. They really think he is the one they have

waited for for hundreds of years. That's where he got his name. The ancient agreement of prophecy of Pahana was that the white man and Hopi would reconcile, correct one another's faults, live side by side, and share in common all the richest of the land and join in faith under one religion that would establish the truth of life in a spirit of universal brotherhood." She paused to think for a moment. *"Perhaps you're right, maybe he could think that as President he could fulfill his prophecy. I sure would like to find out more."*

Tanner handed the dossier to her, *"You are the only operative that can get inside. Go to the reservation, meet his mother and family. Find out about him. Try to get the inside story if you can. This is to be treated as a 'compassionate inquiry' by you, as an anthropologist. You are to meet with him too and to trail him, in part to watch, and in part to protect. Find out whether he is seeking the political arena or just playing with the idea. Become close to him,"* he looked away for a moment, *"anyway you can."*

Maya knew what he was insinuating. *"What do you mean, get him into bed and listen to his pillow talk? Jesus, Tanner."*

Tanner laughed, looking at her again, *"All of our reports say he is celibate. Never had a girlfriend, or woman, that we can find. Don't worry, never had a guy either. We really don't know that much about his personal preferences. Usually, these extremists are very sexually active; as a matter of fact, they can't seem to get enough. He just doesn't seem to fit our usual psychological profile. To us that is a danger signal. Especially since he is so popular. One paper called him, 'God of the Underdog.' We need to know more. We need you to find out for us."*

Tanner stood, moving behind her, placing his hands on her shoulders. They felt very warm, even through her blouse, *"Really something, isn't he? We need to know, Pumpkin. He could be very dangerous to our democracy. Or, he could be our salvation."*

She turned around roughly to face him, *"No, Tanner. The government doesn't think like that. They only think in terms of 'Is he dangerous?' You don't believe in salvation."*

Looking at the photo again, *"Well Tanner, I have to agree that he is quite a hunk, and from all I've read about him, he seems to be very well informed. I'll find out his motives. I just don't know what I'll find. What's this?"*

Included with the dossier was a sealed file, marked *'Top Secret'*. It was quite thick. *"That's a copy of the brief he submitted to the Supreme Court on the Hopi case. Read it, and then destroy it. You know the procedure. But make sure to read it last, after you've gone through the rest of the dossier."*

Tanner prepared to leave. She followed him to the door, *"I just can't promise you anything, Tanner. I'll do my best to get at his motives and plans. What will you do if I find that he really is our salvation? Do you just want that in a verbal report or written?"*

Tanner couldn't tell if she was serious or trying to get under his skin. *"Written, please. And enroute to Arizona on tomorrow's plane,"* he handed her tickets, *"please make a written report on what you know, basics about the Hopis, a little history and a bit about their beliefs, if you please. And try to remember I am a layman on this stuff, okay? Try to make it story-like, so I can understand."* He smiled, leaning down to kiss her cheek and was gone.

Maya felt exhausted suddenly. She was emotionally and physically drained. She had traveled a lot of miles in the past few days. As she sat down again, she picked up the picture.

'This Joseph Pahana, who was he?' She couldn't get past that question in her mind. *'Was he the real Pahana?'*

'Could such a thing really happen?'

CHAPTER 8

ON THE PLANE

Maya carried the dossier with her onto the plane, reviewing some of it again, before starting the report for Tanner. There was information on Joseph Pahana's background, but nothing really out of the ordinary. Except that everything this man did, this Joseph Pahana, was not ordinary.

He seemed to have been a straight-A student all his life, with a line of teachers who wrote adoring, glowing remarks about him. His only side interests were sports and music. Not so strange, remembering a TV program that showed his solid build and almost musical way of talking. What struck her the most about all she read about him was that he seemed *'perfect'*. How could any human being be so perfect? If he was hiding anything, she was determined to find it.

As she shuffled through the thick files, she came upon the copy of the latest Hopi case brief before the Supreme Court. How on earth did Tanner get his hands on that? All Court cases were property of the Court until decisions were rendered. She didn't think anyone got a chance to see them outside of the justices.

"Shows you how much you know", she thought to herself. To give herself a chronology of facts, she decided to scan his other case information first.

For ten years, Joseph Pahana had been an attorney, fighting for the rights of the underdog. There was a listing of some of his clients – individuals, groups, corporations. His win record over those years was generally 52% full victory, 30% negotiated compromises to the agreement of both parties, 12% absolute losses, 6% dead cases or no action. An extremely excellent professional profile.

Maya turned her attention to the cases involving American Indians. Generally, they were involving religious freedom with reclamation of their sacred lands. The litigation intros were similar in most of those cases:

"This nation is heir to a history and tradition of religious diversity that dates from the first settlement of the North American continent…Since that time, adherents of religions too numerous to name have made the U.S. their home, as have those whose beliefs expressly exclude religion. Precisely because of the religious diversity that is our national heritage, the Founders added to the Constitution a Bill of Rights, the very first words of which declare, 'Congress shall make no law respecting an establishment of religion, or prohibiting the free exercise thereof…' Today, these words are recognized as guaranteeing religious liberty or the adherent of a non-Christian faith such as Islam or Judaism. It is settled law that no government official in this Nation may violate these fundamental constitutional rights regarding matters of conscience…The 'establishment of religion' clause of the First Amendment means that neither a state nor federal government can force nor influence a person to go to or remain away from Church (their place of worship) against his will or force him to profess a belief or disbelief in his religion."

Most of the information regarding the 371 treaties that existed between the federal government and various Indian nations was repeated in each case, mainly focusing on the spiritual poverty of being denied the core of their realities (religious freedom).

His arguments to support religious freedom were strong, supported mainly by the First Amendment of the Constitution. The briefs further examined the jurisprudence of original intention, seeking to resurrect the original meaning of constitutional provisions. He quoted the Constitution, how it protects rights for every American, summarizing with *"What is the use of having a written constitution as the 'Supreme Law of the Land' if its provisions can be altered or set aside by Congressional statute?"*

Then he drew a portrait of the American Indian as an intelligent, fully functioning American, *"The American Indian is not a mindless animal, as he is so treated by the white man. This western hemisphere was saturated by the Native Americans' populous in 1500, achieving calendrical mathematics, astronomy, construction, preventative medicine and architecture, all without engendering appreciable environmental disruption. These advanced sociocultural matrices and sustained ecological equilibrium was part of their law – harmony with the environment, the health of which they recognized as an absolute requirement for their continual existence…The beginning of the imbalance to this American world began with the European influx in the 1700's, which has led to the impending destruction of this land's First Americans and the impending environmental catastrophe of their land."*

All the cases had listed numerous treaties and laws that were broken, where land was illegally taken from the Indians. When valuable minerals like ore, gold, coal, etc. were discovered on land previously recognized as owned by Indian tribes, state legislatures had declared all laws of the Indian nations null and void, forbidding Indians to testify in court. Even though Chief Justice John Marshall of the Supreme Court upheld the Cherokee Indians' rights, their land was taken through a fictional new treaty enforced by then President Jackson. The relocation, known as the *'Trail of Tears'* was the beginning of many Indian nations losing not only their land, but the monies that were to be paid them but never were. In some cases there was financial compensation left to help provide jobs and food for the Indians, but, how do you compensate for land that is sacred to the Indian for thousands of generations? They could not relate to the white man's dollar.

There were laws assigning Congress the right to 'terminate' Indian nations, along with laws that placed Indian nations at a civil and criminal jurisdiction level below that of states. Overall, the Indian *aboriginal rights* to at least a portion of their lands was recognized by law, along with the obligation of the U.S. government to ensure a basis for survival of all the indigenous people that the government had subsumed. Laws referred to were Article VI (2) of the Constitution and Article II of the 1948 U.S. Convention of the Prevention and Punishment of the Crime of Genocide, ratified in 1986.

Those case stories were so sad for Maya to read. She closed her eyes a moment, trying to suppress an approaching headache. She leaned back in the seat and let her mind drift to a memory from a few years before. Maya remembered a trip she made to the Black Hills of South Dakota, when she missed meeting Joseph Pahana by just a few hours. There had been an angry meeting between the Lakota Sioux activists and their opposition, the Open Hills Association. The Black Hills had been a sacred place to see visions, that had then become a place for anyone to see the sights. The Bradley Bill had been reintroduced in Congress, and things became pretty stirred up, resulting in some physical confrontations along Spearfish Creek. Tanner had sent her to talk to both groups, and things had finally settled down, especially when they all found out that Joseph Pahana was enroute to meet with them. She remembered that hearing about his coming seemed to be the turning point. She had no reason to wait for him, confident from all she had heard that he would handle things well, better than she could. Before she left, she took some time to really look at the physical beauty of the area, looking at the sacred scenery, Paha Sapa, and found herself wondering about Joseph Pahana, what he was really like. Strange that should stay with her, so many years later.

Maya's eyes opened with a start as she had almost gone to sleep. She sat back again, relaxing for a moment, feeling overwhelmingly tired. This file was full of exceedingly strong arguments against the white man and his government. There were even cited many examples of where the government would either change or completely ignore a law, simply because that law protected the Indian and wouldn't serve the white man's greed.

The only thing that kept her eyes open still was her curiosity about the Hopi Nation VS USA brief. She forced herself to continue reading the files. She noticed another case that was still before the Supreme Court that now had Joseph Pahana's name as the newest counsel. That case called for compensation in the form of money to those Hopi who were forced to fight in World War II – on grounds of religious beliefs as conscientious objectors.

She read, *"The Hopi religion dictates 'If any Hopi show a weapon to anyone to destroy him, that Hopi would not have land in the next world..."* Joseph had provided an addendum to the case, because some of those named had died. The money would be used for purposes like purchasing lifestock or other needful things for that person's clan and village.

The words were mesmerizing Maya, and she found her eyes closing again, as if she were entering a hypnotic state. She felt so relaxed until several voices were being raised near her. She must have fallen asleep. They were landing. She would have to wait to review the Hopi brief and write her own assignment later, after arriving at her motel.

CHAPTER 9

HOOVER BUILDING

"What are you reading this time, Weatherford? Jesus, you look scared to death."

Peter Weatherford didn't want to be where he was, seated at his desk, pretending to be an F.B.I. agent. He was just getting over some kind of flu bug, at least he hoped that was all it was. And that he was going to recover. He put the newspaper down and looked at his partner. Weatherford didn't enjoy being belittled, especially by Ralph K. Niehardt, stubborn and argumentative F.B.I. man, *'Mister Stickler-for-Details'*.

"Nothing, just reading the paper. And, if it's any of your business, I'd rather be home in bed on drugs. I don't feel good. Okay? Now, will you leave it alone? Go find someone else to bother." He held the paper back up, held higher to cover his face, so Niehardt would maybe take the hint.

The two men were a good partnership, balancing out one another's strengths and weaknesses. Waterford had a tendency to be shy and impetuous, and sloppy on details. Niehardt made up for that. And Weatherford sometimes could get Niehardt to ease a little. Not much, but just enough. Sometimes.

They had been dormitory roomies at the Farm, each in military training for special operations. They had been together 24 hours a day for 16 weeks. Three years later, they were still planning their futures together and selected the F.B.I. over the C.I.A., wanting to focus on domestic operations. They were good for one another and had a good record after five years at the F.B.I.. Both still single, neither was very good at keeping a woman in his life. Weatherford was too insecure. Niehardt was too secure.

Niehardt, needing to meet his quota for being an asshole on this particular day, decided to continue needling his partner. *"Don't tell me you think you have' IT'! How many hours do you think you have left to live, Petie? Poor baby*!" And he proceeded to grab the newspaper out of Weatherford's hands.

"Come on, Ralph. Cut it out! Don't make fun of such a serious issue, damn it! And besides, if I had it, I sure wouldn't be sitting here now."

"Oh, you're just nuts, Petie. A real worry wart. Hypochondriac! Pure fruitcake."

"How do you know I'm nuts? Huh? Where's the proof?" Weatherford's pale face was now flushed.

"I would say that behavioral patterns are limited, but acceptable evidence."

"Gentlemen, please! Would you mind getting serious for a moment and join me in a meeting?" Elliott Tanner was used to these two. But, standing with his hands on his hips, he wanted them to know there were some serious activities going on around them. *"Fifth floor conference room. Five minutes. Jackets please."*

As Peter Weatherford straightened his tie and reached for his jacket, he continued to glance at page one. The subject was important enough to warrant two separate front-page stories. One was the latest report out of the Atlanta headquarters of the Center of Disease Control. The other was the World Health Network. The subject was one and the same – the latest killer disease, which had now reached the U.S. There had been thousands of cases in New York City, Miami, Chicago and Los Angeles. Just all of a sudden appeared, five weeks earlier. No one knew the cause. Virus. Bacteria. Flea bite. No one even knew what it was yet. All they knew was that within 48 to 72 hours, it killed. Everyone it infected. Small villages in Europe and Africa had become completely depopulated. Ghost towns. Death tolls were adding up.

Almost one million deaths. People were scared. Health experts were frantic. Peter Weatherford felt chills.

When he looked up and saw Ralph's frown, he managed a shrug and threw the paper into the trash.

The conference room on the fifth floor of the Hoover Building felt humid and uncomfortable. The square-shaped room held a large mahogany table with twenty chairs along each side and had a cheap government chandelier five feet above the table.

Weatherford and Niehardt weren't sure where to sit, so they stood near the end of the table where Tanner was already sitting, shuffling papers.

The President's Chief of Staff, Joel Wattenberg, burst into the room, exploding the space surrounding him. He appeared to be moving in double-time today, seemingly anxious to meet and then move on. He put his briefcase on a chair, but remained standing as usual, arms folded. He stared at Tanner, who had yet to look up. Wattenberg never waited to be acknowledged and decided to take over, as usual. *"Shall we get started?"* He looked at the two agents, unfolded his arms just long enough to gesture in the direction of two of the chairs, indicating for them to sit.

Then he folded his arms again and stood, poised and waiting like a sentry who couldn't wait to fire. *"Damn it, Tanner, I don't have all day."*

Tanner looked up almost nonchalantly. He didn't like Wattenberg's type and refused to play his games. He knew he would have little input into this meeting, so he introduced everyone, then sat back in his chair, glancing at the papers in front of him and scribbled some notes on his legal pad.

As expected, Wattenberg took over. *"Gentlemen,"* looking at the agents, *"we have an assignment for you. By we – I am referring to the President of the United States and myself."* He reached into his case, took out two manila folders and tossed them in front of the two agents. *"You can read these after our meeting. Generally, Mr. Weatherford and Mr. Niehardt, we want you to follow the two gentlemen whose pictures are in these files. One is Joseph Pahana, the other is his fellow Indian sidekick John Saxon, a sort of Tonto-type without the feathers. Your mission is to keep a diary of where they go, who they see. I want you to report to me directly every two days, giving me a verbal report. My private phoneline is written in the file along with the time to call. I shall tell you each step as we go along. You will report to me and only me. Your written diary is to be faxed both to Tanner here and to the President, whose fax number is also inside the file. This subject is of the highest priority – top secret. While you are on this mission, no personal contacts with anyone. And no one but the people in this room are to know your whereabouts. Is that clear?"*

Both men nodded to Wattenberg but looked questioningly over to Tanner. Not reporting to their FBI superior was highly irregular. They felt a need for confirmation. Tanner was reading something and seemed to be paying no attention.

"Sir?" Niehardt needed to make sure. *"Will we be operating 'naked', sir?"* (meaning without any other assistance)

Tanner looked up at last, *"Pretty much, guys. Anything irregular happens, you call me as well as Wattenberg. Otherwise, do exactly as he says. After all, this job is directly for the President. We do have an operative undercover – she is not a lady to compromise the situation but is like you – our agent. Only difference is Pahana thinks she is just an interesting anthropologist, studying his Indian culture. So make sure you protect her. I'll let her know we have you nearby."*

"No!!" shouted Wattenberg, *"She is NOT to know about them. They are to maintain surveillance, but out of sight! Understand?"*

"I see," was all Tanner would say. He didn't like this whole thing. No one but O'Toole knew that he had someone already

trailing Pahana and watching out for Maya. He looked at his two agents, *"You will have the usual 'music box' equipment. Meet me in my office for the issuance and to review the regs."* He rose from his chair, pushing his papers into a carryable pile, *"If you will excuse me, I have a meeting."*

Wattenberg felt he had one more thing to say, ignoring Tanner, *"I reward my friends and I punish my enemies. That's how you survive in politics. You dance with the ones that brought you. So, dance with me and you two will be fine. And whether you realize it or not, gentlemen, you are involved shit-deep in the world of politics."*

Tanner was halfway out the door and hearing this thought to himself that this guy is really on an ego trip. And fairly nuts, too.

CHAPTER 10

ARIZONA

As her plane landed, Maya found she felt refreshed in spirit and physically but with nervous energy. She had never had a chance to visit the Hopi Reservation and looked forward to it. For many reasons. She hadn't felt such anticipation in several years and was grateful for the assignment.

She found her rental Jeep and decided to drive around a little before heading out to the reservation. She had just been given an extra three hours from the trip out West and headed south for about twenty minutes to revisit Sedona.

It was still mid-morning and the sky was a proper Arizona blue as she raced south on Route 17, leaving pine trees behind, anticipating the supreme beauty soon to dazzle her eyes and stir her soul. There was something quite mystical about the red rock area that was not quite of this world.

As soon as Maya entered the small resort community, with its backdrop of the grand temples of Sedona's Red Rock Country, she remembered her first visit here. And she found herself repeating the same *'fever'* she had experienced then, several years before. It was like following a linkage that is unimaginably ancient. Most of the thin layers of dark, light and red rock that form Sedona's phantasmagoria of mesas, buttes and pinnacles are the very same layers that, in thicker form, are found in the upper chapters of the Grand Canyon's vertical geology text and also make up the entire Colorado Plateau. But here, below the plateau's southern edge, called the Mogollon Rim, some unique event happened long ago, depositing an especially thick, bright, red and (in places) erosion-resistant layer. This layer, now carved into serene and awesome shapes by wind and water, is what the locals really mean when they talk about visitors coming down with *'red rock fever'*, the urge to drop everything and move in.

Maya found a spot to pull off the road with a view of the valley where it looked wide open and profoundly secret, superimposed above by the towering red rocks. Silent, stoic, suggesting a kind of serene eternity, with blankets of pinon, juniper and Arizona cypress reaching up into crevices, clinging and prostrate. Here and there were flat terraces of red rimrock, curved and smooth, with small circular depressions where the rock breaks off in thin layers. She remembered standing in this same spot before, at the end of a day, feeling her heart stir as the sun made flamboyant love to those patient, beckoning rocks.

She had discovered old Indian ruins, mostly small ones, in the cliffs and caves around Sedona, and had seen the large, once teeming pueblos in the outlying lands. The Hopi say the Sinagua, who had lived there, were early clans who left the salubrious valleys about 1300 AD because their prophecies told them to.

Maya shook the memories from her head and started her drive back to Flagstaff along Oak Creek, which sluices down the deep canyon from near Flagstaff, sweeping through Sedona into the Verde River to the south. The scenery changed during the fifteen-minute drive, from churning rapids and serene pools with red sandstone set off against unexpected greenery, to lusher greenery of tall pines, alternating sun and shade over steep gorges. Along the road that crisscrosses the creek were a host of lodges and camping grounds largely hidden in the trees under the towering canyon walls. A part of her longed to investigate – so much to see, such little time.

As she reached Flagstaff searching for her route to travel northeast, Maya looked to her left to mentally greet the San Francisco Mountains, peaks still covered with snow. The Kachina spirits were said to dwell there.

Today's Hopi Reservation was uniquely surrounded by another reservation, the much larger Navajo Nation. The Hopi land extended from the eerily beautiful Painted Desert on the south to high pine and pinyon country on the north. Within this swatch of land were deserts of multi-colored sand, great sand dunes, gulches, washes, canyons, high rise buttes, mesas, grasslands and forests of juniper and pine. Well over half of the land was made up of treeless, windswept valleys and plains broken in many places by spectacular mesas and equally spectacular canyons. Arizona Highway 264 (Navajo Route 3) bisected the Hopi Reservation on an east-west axis, skirting or passing over each of the three Hopi mesas.

When Maya arrived at her room at the Cultural Center on the second mesa, it was late morning and she wanted to rest a little before driving to the village to meet Joseph Pahana's mother. She took a quick shower and ate a small lunch while writing out a little history for Tanner. Then she could mail it overnight before she went '*visiting*'.

As she pulled out her portable laptop computer, she thought about whether she would believe it if she found Joseph Pahana was the salvation for mankind. She had never tested her faith before. Her faith in God, the Creator and her heritage of being an Indian, albeit a Sioux Indian. As she collected her thoughts, she recalled how the Hopi was one of the more mystic Indian tribes.

"Report on History of the Hopis – the Oldest People of the Americas?" Good title. She must make sure to mix the myths with logical history. The F.B.I. recognized logic. They only asked your opinion based on that. And so she wrote…

"Finds made throughout America and dated by carbon-14 tests prove that man existed in America at least 20,000 and possibly 30,000 years ago. New blood-group studies of living Indians may push this horizon back still more. The purest 0 groups in the world have been found among Indians. If these Indians are

direct descendants of the people of 20,000 years ago, they may be the oldest race which first peopled this continent.

"Anthropology asserts that the Hopis were members of the Shoshonean branch of the Uto-Aztecan language family of Mongoloids, who migrated to America by way of the Bering Strait crossing, arriving in the Southwest about 700 AD. Other tribal groups include the Ute, Kiowa and Tanoan Pueblo in the U.S., and the Yaqui, Tarahumara and Aztec in Mexico.

"This is far afield from Hopi tradition, which asserts that the Hopi came much earlier, that they did not enter this continent through the Back Door to the North – via Bering Strait. That the Place of Emergence was 'down below' in the tropical South, somewhere in Middle America.

She felt that she shouldn't get too long on the technical facts and lose those who would be reading her report, so she left out quite a bit. She next needed to add in some of their belief history, to lead up to discussing Joseph Pahana.

"The bearded white gods of the Mayas, Toltecs and Aztecs came from Asia in 323 BC. An older book postulates a large influx of Mongolians into Mexico in 668 AD and 1175 AD. These literary conjectures seem to conform with native myth. The Popul Vuh, Sacred Book of the Quiche Maya in Yucatan follows these same Mongolian travels, as well as similarities to Hopi legends.

"Middle America was the hub of life in the New World, the new Fourth World, with its magnificent stone cities, pyramid-temples, dominating priesthoods, abstract symbolism and a calendar more accurate than the one we now use – here at the Place of Emergence where the Hopis began their continental migrations.

"Without doubt the Hopis were once part of this great complex, whose perimeter was gradually extended northward through Chihuahua to the four corners area of the southwest U.S.

"The Hopis believe that the early Mayas, Toltecs and Aztecs were aberrant Hopi clans who failed to complete their fourfold migrations, remaining in Middle America to build mighty cities which perished because they failed to perpetuate their ordained religious pattern. (According to Hopi pattern, their migrations were to go North, South, East and West in a cross from the four corners area of our Southwest.)

"All of the great pueblos in the southwestern area were built between 700 and 1100 AD. Their period of greatest occupancy was roughly from 1000 to 1300 AD, most of them having been abandoned shortly before and during the Great Drought from 1276 to 1299 AD. This period coincides with the establishment of the first Hopi villages on the three Hopi mesas in Arizona. The earliest date established for ruins below the present village of Oraibi is 1150 AD, which makes it the oldest continuously occupied settlement in the United States."

Maya hoped that these types of historical details would at least spark a small amount of respect in those at the Bureau and in the government who would be reading this. Alas, our government has never shown very much respect for the Native American, something which Maya would like to see change. Perhaps she was a little biased about this. She continued her report.

"The clan is still the heart of Hopi society. Each is composed of several families, the members of each family being related through matrilineal descent and taking the clan name of the mother. Each clan has a name – usually that of a bird, beast, or other living entity. Each also has a special guardian spirit, represented by a stone or wood fetish. Most of the important clans possess a ritual or complete ceremony whose power benefits all the community. Land allotments are held in the name of the clan. There are approximately twelve recognized clans. Some have clan-successive groups within, for instance, the Parrot Clan has three groups – Crow, Rabbit and Tobacco.

"The Bear Clan is acknowledged the leading Hopi clan – it lays out the life plan for the year in the great Soyal ceremony, and the Village Chief of Oraibi must be a member of the Bear Clan. The most important clans are the Bear, Parrot, Eagle and Badger, whose chiefs represent the four directions they entered Oraibi after their migrations.

Maya paused for a few moments to collect her thoughts. She must include information on the Pahana. Hopefully after the information included in this report, the readers may understand more about why his people believe in him so much. At least, she will be getting their attention.

"The coming of the Hopi 'lost white brother', Pahana, like the return of the Mayas' bearded white god Kukulcan, the Toltecan and Aztecan Quetzalcoatl, was a myth common throughout all pre-Columbian America. This event was long hailed by prophecy.

"The Hopis have long anticipated his coming. Every year in Oraibi, on the last day of Soyal, a line was drawn across the six-foot-long stick kept in the custody of the Bear Clan to mark the time of his arrival. The true Pahana, the symbol of all America's deep-rooted need and vision of the universal brotherhood of man, was yet to come.

"Today, the People of Peace are compressed upon a tiny Hopi 'island' in a great Navajo sea bounded by the continental shores of white supremacy. Despite pressures from without and discord within, they still maintain their traditional concept of full sovereignty.

"Who was their leader? The Fire Clan was dominant in their First World; the Spider Clan in the Second World; the Bow Clan in the Third World; and the Bear Clan in the Fourth. And they say he is the one, this Joseph Pahana. Is he? Is he the proclaimed Pahana – a man supposedly born of white man and Hopi woman, but whose skin is paler than Indian skin, and his

eyes light brown instead of dark brown/black? And is he who he says he is, who they say he is? My next report will begin to address that question."

"End of Report."

There was so much she didn't know. Written records of these Indians only went so far. She knew a little about the Four Worlds but needed to know so much more. But at least this much should satisfy them, she hoped. Was it necessary to go into further detail about the history of the previous three worlds of the Hopi? Even after she knew more, she doubted they would care or really understand. As she put her computer away and sat back to relax a moment, her mind drifted back over what she had read about their history. She was going to have to learn so much from these people that they haven't told others. Perhaps Joseph Pahana's mother and other members of their family and friends could tell her.

Until she knew whether he was really a savior or not, she would word her reports to Tanner very carefully, not revealing all of her feelings and knowledge until the end report. After she knew for sure.

Before heading to the village, Maya drove to a nearby wide flat ledge, overlooking the valley she had crossed earlier. In the distance stood the San Francisco Peaks. *"Hello again…"*

She looked around the ledge where she stood, noticing a few signs of simple Hopi shrines nearby, including one close to her, a pile of yellow rocks about two-and-a-half feet high, with a weathered stick protruding from the top. Tied to the stick with a bit of string was a spotted, buff-and-white feather. This shrine's prayer-feather rose and floated on some imperceptible breeze, a paahos, carrying a message up to the sky. She looked up, hearing voices but seeing no one. There were other feathers all around her, tied to jackpines or small dry clumps of scrub. This simple rock pile was sacred to the Hopi, as a church or cathedral would be to a Christian. Each shrine had a guardian spirit, represented by the feather, a prayer for rain, for peace, for friendship, for continuation of the Hopi way of being respectful citizens of this, the Fourth World, to which the Hopi were led after three previous worlds had been destroyed by corruption. Again, she heard voices, and seeing no one thought perhaps there were people nearby, hidden by the rocks. So, she just shrugged it off.

Maya knew it was time to go – she felt an almost-physical pull towards the rental Jeep. She stopped before climbing behind the wheel and looked once more towards the faraway snowcapped mountains gleaming in the sunshine.

There was an eagle banking against a cloudy horizon and she watched it dive near the promontory where she had just been standing, then fly off in the direction she was to go, all while repeating a screeching call. Was he calling her to follow? She shook her head to clear it of these strange thoughts, so she could concentrate on more tangible things. She needed to remind herself she was not here on a mystical journey, but on an investigative assignment.

"Watch out, girl, you're getting a little carried away," she said out loud to herself.

CHAPTER 11

HOPI RESERVATION

Maya wanted to drive through Shungopovi before Mishongonovi, where Pahana's mother lived with relatives. In the pearly light of a half-overcast afternoon, it was easy to see the casual overlapping of cultures in Shungopovi, the oldest of Hopi villages and the largest of the three on Second Mesa. Clan symbols coexisted with American flags, while houses with outdoor bread ovens, looking a bit like beehives made of rock, boasted a new pickup truck here and there. The setting was a mixture of battered trailers and cinder-block huts, with old-style mud-brick houses built around two swept-earth plazas that looked out over the desert to a line of fantastical buttes.

She had apparently arrived just in time for a ceremony. Curious, Maya felt compelled to stay and watch. She found a seat on a concrete block next to a young Indian family, who had signaled for her to join them. It was impolite to talk during the ceremony, but since it hadn't begun yet, she quietly asked what dance this would be. An older woman, perhaps the grandmother, answered her in hushed tones, *"You see, this is the end of the pilgrimage for spruce. Our men have gone and selected the spruce and prayed, returning to the kiva with the trees and branches, and the trees were planted in the kisonvi. Our men have been denied water for two days and have done their first Home Dance, or Niman Kachina, at sunrise today."*

Maya tried to recall some of the basics she had studied about the Hopi ceremonial ritual, to prepare herself mentally and perhaps emotionally for what she would be seeing.

Mass prayer was at the root of their major ceremonies – more than reciting of words, but to desire and will the essentials of

72

their life – security, abundant crops, health, long life, and children. The prayer was given added strength by the number of participants. All must maintain correct thoughts and desires. All must be attentive and participate in spirit.

A multitude of details clothed the ceremonies, both the public parts in the plaza and the closed enactments in the kiva. All was fixed in tradition – details of the costumes, training of the participants. Everything had a meaning.

There were usually many masked figures representing the kachina spirits, called up from an old sleep. A man would feel strong, uplifting powers in his portrayal of a spirit that he normally wouldn't have in daily life. Although these elaborate rites were so firmly entrenched in Hopi religion, the Hopi never set apart a special class of priests from other human beings, such as the Buddhist priests of Tibet and other Oriental countries. They were instead normal people, respected because of their character and attainments, not the reverse where position conferred recognition.

All young people received a unified training toward a happy and useful life, with no formal distinction between practical affairs and spiritual, because those two were indissolubly related. All the ceremonies reinforced the Hopi way – a course of conduct leading to well-being and happiness. It had a certain parallel in the Road to Nirvana as conceived by Gautama more than 2,000 years ago – right speech, conduct, aims, effort and state of mind. It coincided with many of the Ten Commandments. A Hopi would seek '*a good heart*,' aware that he was part of a great, immortal spirit world.

The ceremony began, as the kachinas came in single file through the narrow streets into the plaza. The Powamu Chief, unmasked, wearing a single eagle feather and an embroidered kilt, led the Kachina Father and his assistant, wearing plain kilts, followed by some thirty '*hemis*' kachinas and eight kachina-manas. '*Hemis*' meant '*far-away*', from which the kachinas came and to which they will return. Their bodies were painted black with white nakwach symbols on the breast and back. Spruce branches hung from the belts of their kirtles and twigs were stuck in their blue arm bands. In the right hand each carried a rattle and black yarn tied to the wrist. In the left hand, each carried a twig of spruce and a downy feather. Deer-hoof and turtle-shell rattles were worn on the right leg, a strap of bells on the left. Most notable was the distinctive headdress. Above a ruff of spruce around the throat, the face mask was painted yellow on the left side, blue on the right, above rose a blue cloud-terrace tablita or tiara tufted with heads of white wheat and downy eagle feathers, topped by two eagle-tail and two parrot feathers symbolizing the kasknuna, the parrot's power of warmth. Just above the face a red rainbow arched over a field of white painted with a frog or butterfly. In some rituals, there would be different kachina masks, but in Niman, all the masks were the same.

The eight kachina-manas wore bright orange face masks and the hair whorls ceremonially worn by unmarried Hopi maidens, a black manta, a red and white blanket, and white deerskin boots. Each carried a pumpkin shell, notched stick, and the scapula bone of a sheep or deer, to use for music.

They stood silently while the Powamu Chief sprinkled each with cornmeal from a sack worn on his breast. The Kachina Father seemed to be encouraging them with talk. Then suddenly, the leader of the kachinas, standing in the middle of the line, shook his rattle. Powerful legs lifted and stamped, and the low, strong voices broke into song – a day-long song and dance, beautiful and compelling.

Maya felt there was something different about the kachina leader but couldn't quite figure what it was. Perhaps it was because he seemed stronger, huskier in build than the others. His body was lean muscle, muscle that moved with the kind of intensity and power that comes only to those who work hard and take care of themselves.

Symbolically, they danced, curving their northern line west

and south, breaking a circle before it was formed as the pattern of life was broken and the First World destroyed. The dancers then curved toward the south, breaking the pattern of life in the Second World. Moving to the south side and curving east, they repeated the procedure representing the Third World. With each section of the song and dance, they sang louder and stamped their feet more powerfully. The kachinas were struggling to maintain the proper balance in the Fourth World and were working hard to lift up the performance and the thoughts of the people watching.

Maya looked around, seeing only a few dozen people watching the dance. Most seemed to be village people, older men and women, young mothers holding infants, and the children. She was sure the children had witnessed the dance many times, but their faces showed their fascination with dark eyes huge and shining.

Soon their faces showed delight, as the kachinas, sweating and shiny from dancing hard in the sun, began searching out the children with gifts – the first corn from the fields, cattails, rolls of red, white and blue piki, bows and arrows, plaques, and kachina dolls and toy bows for the youngest children.

Maya was surprised to see the kachina leader move towards her with a gift. He stopped before her, seemed to nod his head, handing her the doll. Maya couldn't take her eyes away from him. He was painted black like the others but there was still a feeling she had about him being different. She finally looked at the doll after he had turned and moved away rhythmically, as if he were dancing.

She recognized the figure she was holding as a Humis Kachinamana, usually representing the paired kachina's sister or sweetheart. Her doll wore a black dress, white cape with red stripes, deerskin boots and her hair was coiled in an older manner to represent an unmarried maiden. The facial mask was yellow, with downy eagle feather trim along the bottom. There was a painted feather on top, with bands of various colors. She felt movement around her and looked up to see everyone moving about the plaza as though the dance was over.

The grandmother sat down next to Maya smiling at her. She reached over and touched the top feather. "*This doll is significant as it means he is asking to be with you tonight.*" Seeing Maya's expression, she laughed, "*Yes, in ancient times, it was the way he would show he had selected you. But today he is asking to spend time with you just getting acquainted.*"

Maya felt embarrassed. "*But, I am on my way to Mishongonovi. I am expected there.*"

The grandmother seemed confused, "*But that is where you will find him. His family is there.*" She looked at Maya with large, dark brown eyes that said far more than she would ever reveal. "*We were lucky to have him here – he lives in Washington, D.C. now. He is a very well-loved man, our Joseph, loved by the white man as well as the Indian. He will find you.*"

As the woman smiled and walked away, Maya felt dazed, realizing what had happened. "*Joseph. Could it be?*" Looking at the doll in her hands, she walked back to the Jeep.

CHAPTER 12

MISHONGONOVI

Maya arrived at Mishongonovi and parked her Jeep near the edge of the pueblo village. She noticed how the village structures were constructed mainly of shaped sandstone blocks bound together with a minimum of mortar, leaning this way and that, almost mindless of gravity. Like a mist, an aura of oldness hung over the pueblos. Visiting them was like walking through the pages of a history book. She ran the images through her mind, meticulously, to remember everything, forget nothing, imprinting all of it forever, like tribesmen passing down an oral history through the generations. There was much about this place that suggested the peacefulness she had felt in the Mayan village.

The things in life that were important to the white man were not to the Hopi. The world of the cities was a long way from the Hopi world. The realm of new and complex inventions was interesting to them, but not vital. The devastating events on other continents, the wars and prospects of wars, the complexities of conflicting civilizations were alien. Being terrible and destructive, they should not be thought about too much.

To a Hopi, the affairs of his own household and those of his neighbors and his village, the raising and harvesting of crops, the practice of traditional crafts, the preparation for ceremonies and participation in them, the visits to and from relatives – these were the matters which commanded interest. They were close at hand, understandable, and constructive. They were worth thinking about.

A sound caught Maya's attention. It was like the "*clop,*

clop" of a burro, but the sound appeared hollow and as if made by tin or sheet iron. Maya turned around and saw the cause of the sound. The *'burro'* was a small boy moving along at a brisk pace on all fours. In each hand, he held an empty tin can. These extended his arms to permit fast progress while at the same time producing a satisfactory sound. A still smaller boy was riding on the back of this *'burro'*, his legs clasping his mount tightly. In his hand he carried a two-foot length of string which served as an adequate imitation of a whip. They were having a good time. A Hopi boy has few mechanical toys, certainly no mechanical trains. A tin-can burro was more realistic, costing nothing to acquire and like a burro himself is economical in upkeep.

Smiling to herself, impressed with the creativity of the boys, she continued walking along the dusty pueblo street past centuries-old houses. Maya thought about other differences in the Hopi family from the white man's world. A Hopi household was a self-directing group, the members of which seem to achieve an automatic coordination of their activities. No one tells the others what they should do, or when, or how. No one exercised authority. The various members seemed to fall naturally into a pattern in which the abilities of the individual and the needs of the household were satisfactorily served – a pattern which probably was evolved so long ago that it required no direction and was accepted without question.

Maya soon found the old house she was searching for. She had been told that it was the one with a two-foot-high stone wall, running around three sides of the house. There was a man standing, surveying the wall, who turned around and greeted her. *"Ah, you are here. What do you think of my wall?"* Maya wasn't sure she was the one he expected and didn't know who he was. So she just smiled and nodded, adding *"I'm Maya Chardon."* He came over and took her hand in his calloused, dry, dusty one, *"And I am Hon'hoya, Joseph's grandfather. My name means 'Little Bear'."*

His lean muscular frame belying his elderly years, his steely eyes and tanned leather-lined face perhaps confirming a number of them, he explained that he was busy at work building an addition to his house. It would be an enlargement, rather than an extra room. He had started it several weeks before, but he was not trying to complete it on any set schedule. When there was suitable opportunity, he prepared sand and clay mortar and laid up some more stones.

"When I have it as high as the house," he said, *"I'll put on the roof and take out the wall where this joins the house. That way, I'll make the room in there a big one. Then when other members of our family come to see us, when there is a ceremony, we can have many all together in the house."*

As they stood outside the door to the house, Hon'hoya explained what the procedure would be for entering. You must always knock. The owner will answer with a greeting to come in, which refers to both you, the visible and the invisible spirit beside you. After the door is opened, you would hear another greeting, which again welcomed you '*both*'.

He knocked on the door, then they heard, *"Pe'o ia'a."* As they stepped into the darker interior of the house, someone said, *"Ie'se e."* At last Maya was to meet Joseph Pahana's mother. It took only a moment for her eyes to adjust to the darkness of the house, and she saw an older woman, seated on a mat on the floor, finishing the last coils of a basket. Her hair was gray, pulled back away from her face and her eyes were almost shut as she smiled at Maya. Her dress was colorful, and she wore a gray sweater, although the weather was warm. She reached out her hand, indicating Maya to sit on a stool next to her. Maya looked around and saw that Hon'hoya had quietly left. There were only two rooms. With the addition, it would still have two rooms, but there would be more fun in having a big room than in possessing a third.

"Maya, welcome to our house. This is our family, all of

Joseph's cousins and aunts." She indicated to several women and girls that were scurrying about looking very busy. *"I am Joseph Pahana's mother, Kwa'ngwa mana, which means Sweet Maiden. I have been waiting to meet you, ever since my son told me you would be coming."*

Maya couldn't understand what she meant. How did Joseph Pahana know she was coming? They had told no one, except in making arrangements for her at the Cultural Center, and sending word she was here as an Anthropologist, who was interested in the Hopi people. It was supposed to be an under-cover investigation. She would have to talk to Tanner about a possible leak.

"I didn't know that Joseph knew I was coming to see you," said Maya. *"When did he tell you?"*

"He said you would be coming months ago. You see, Maya, my son knows all, way before it happens. Even way before it is even planned. It is what you call destiny. He even knew who you were."

"What did he tell you about me?"

"He said you were also a mix of Indian and proud of it. He also said you studied many Indian cultures, not just ours. He told us of your help with the Lakota Indian problems in the Black Hills. Also he said you would be very important to our future. I did not ask more. He did not tell me more. That is all I needed to know."

Joseph's mother was a woman with an aging face that must have been beautiful once. As she talked, Kwa'ngwa mana kept working on her basket, which was very attractive. Its design interesting, its colors soft and pleasing. She worked with a sure touch, thrusting the awl through a coil at just the right angle to maintain the symmetry of the basket, drawing the yucca binder smoothly tight. She was unhurried and seemed to enjoy her work.

Maya looked at the others that were closeby. A ten-year-old-child, seated beside Kwa'ngwa mana was learning the craft and finding it required practice and experience. The small disk which she was making, intended to be the flat base of a plaque or basket, was acquiring a warped contour which would not do. For her, the awl thrust was not yet quite what it should be, but she also was patient and unhurried. The next one would turn out better.

The girl's mother knelt behind one of the metates, the one with the finer grain, and proceeded with the final grinding of the heap of blue cornmeal waiting at its base. Deftly she swept part of the meal onto the stone with her slender brush of hairgrass and ground it with the stone mano held in her two hands. Later the meal would be used in making piki, for today was the final day of the Niman ceremony, and a supply of piki would be needed. Relatives would be arriving from another village and would be visiting the household.

Kwa'ngwa mana smiled at Maya, *"I know why you have come. I would like to tell you about my son. Joseph was born on August 11, 1960, a significant day for all of us and a significant year. On this day also, one of your big city museum's people unearthed a tiponi from an ancient ruin near Springville, Arizona. The image was 9" high, carved from sandstone, painted with vertical stripes of orange, green, blue and black, with its right arm missing. This was a fetish of stone representing the diety and belonging to the clan. It is seldom brought out into the open and is not generally known, being reserved for ritual use in the kiva. The image was of Panaiyoikyasi, Short Rainbow, representing a spiritual tie among the Water Clans, specifically the Short Well and Deep Well Clans at that site. It was important, of course, in your field, as a discovery. But it was important to us, as it was representative of the first sign of many, showing the beginning of spiritual ties among the Hopi people."*

"Why was the year 1960 important?"

"The Bear Clan was first to complete all four legs of its

81

*migration and settled the land first. Here between the Rio Grande
and the Colorado Rivers. A member of this clan always serves as
Village Chief, and is regarded as the father of Oraibi, just as the
Parrot Clan is considered the mother. The Chief Tawakwaptiwa of
the Bear Clan was married to a woman of the Parrot Clan. They
were symbolically the father and mother of Oraibi. According to
Hopi prophecy, this was the last couple to unite the two clans.
When the Chief died in 1960, Oraibi was left without proper
parents – an omen of the end of Oraibi. But also the beginning of
a new journey for my people. Also that was the year we stopped
using the staff in the ceremony that would tell us when Pahana
would appear. That was the first year that we couldn't read the
signs. So we stopped using it. That was the year our Pahana was
born."*

Maya looked with wonder upon this old woman, an Indian
interpreting the Indian world, providing an authentic angle on the
past. Whenever she said the word *"we"*, she meant more than just
this generation, she was talking about every generation back to
the first one. William Faulkner said that once about another
enigmatic society, the South, *"The past is not dead. It isn't even
past."* That was the way the Hopi felt.

"There is more," said Kwa'ngwa mana. *"Our prophecy tells
us he would be a white man. Joseph is of the white man, as well
as of the Hopi. And his skin is paler than usual, as are his eyes.
And he had been very well educated in the white man's world.
But, most significantly, when he was born, we didn't know all of
this at first. You see, a baby is like a plant that has started to grow
from a seed. It must be protected in just the same way. It needs
ten days that are required when a little plant is sent from a seed
up to the surface of the ground, and another ten days the sun
must not shine on a new plant. We covered the windows of our
house, placed an ear of perfect corn whose tip ends in four full
kernels for his Corn Mother, beside him. This was for twenty days.
He was kept in darkness, as is our way, for this time. You see, for
while his newborn body was of this world, he was still under the*

protection of his universal parents. We prepared his body with cedar brewed water, and cedar ashes for the first three days. Then we alternated cornmeal and ashes, while I drank a little of the cedar water each day. During this, his grandfather, as is custom, wove a blanket for him, a soft, warm square, done in broad white and black bars, forming a checkered pattern.

"On the morning of the twentieth day, while still dark, all of the aunts came, each carrying a Corn Mother, wishing to be his godmother. First he was bathed, then I held him in my left arm, took up the Corn Mother that had been with him and passed it over him four times from navel upward to his head. I named him, wished him a long life, and a healthy life. Then I wished him a productive life in his work. We left the house, walking toward the east to meet the sun and prayed. As I held him up to the horizon, showing Father Sun his child, I noticed the pallor of his skin and eyes. I didn't become alarmed, I just noted it. We completed the cornmeal path toward the sun and named him Tip'si ta'wa, Baby of the Sun, because of his light color. He now belonged to our family and to the earth.

"As we were making ready for his birth celebration, I took a closer look at his body. You see, in our darkened house for those twenty days, I couldn't see him that well. I just knew he was a boy child. I noticed other, significant markings on his body. He had been born with wound scars on his body, the scars from the migration test given by the eagle. There was one near his eye, and on each side of his body, left side below the heart, right side below the waist. Those tests were to prove power and strength to the eagle. The eagle is conqueror of air and master of height, power of space above, representing loftiness of spirit. Born with those scars means this child had the spirits within him, and that his messages passed through the eagle directly to the Creator. In other words, his marks and his light skin, being of the white man and Hopi, meant he was the Pahana. Of that we have no doubt."

A man's voice behind Maya added, *"He hears voices*

others do not hear, sees visions that confirm his dreams." As Maya turned to look at the man, he left before she could see who he was.

"That is Na'moki, our medicine man. He knows all of which we speak," said Kwa'ngwa mana.

"When did he receive his name Joseph Pahana?"

"Upon his first initiation into the religious society he was renamed, and fully recognized as the Pahana. We have watched his allegiance to the great universe grow as he has grown. You see, when you are seven or eight years old, the child learns that he has human parents, but also his real parents were the universal entities who had created him through them. His Mother Earth, from whose flesh all are born, and his Father Sun, the solar god who gives life to all the universe."

She finished talking and rose to leave the room. Maya sat and waited, noticing that someone had removed the white cloth that covered a dozen round loaves of bread arrayed on the table. They looked invitingly brown and crusty. She knew that they had been baked in an outdoor oven and that they had been made in preparation for the Niman. The guests and relatives would expect this bread and find special enjoyment in it. Just as they would count on mutton stew and piki and would expect the food to be placed on a mat on the floor, around which they would gather on other mats.

Kwa'ngwa mana was still gone, probably maintaining the slow fire under the piki stone. The young mother was making ready a vessel of boiling hot water with which to make batter for the piki. The girl had started a new base for a coiled basket and was working at it thoughtfully, estimating with care the proper angle for the awl. The air was still and quiet, and Maya found herself feeling very relaxed.

She investigated the room with her eyes. This was a house

built a hundred or more years ago, and now little changed except for the to-be addition. The two rooms were small. Its windows looked out upon a village street where many generations of children have played and grown up together. In the living room, bunches of roasted and dried ears of sweet corn hung along the top of a wall. In the winter, two walls would be occupied by these. Now only a few bunches remained, since the new crop was not ready yet. Here and there a downy feather from an eagle hung from a short cotton string fastened to a small stick that was thrust into the closely-packed brush over a ceiling beam – gifts from the winter solstice ceremony to signify a blessing on the house and its occupants. A coiled plaque decorated one of the walls. Two kachina dolls gave a gay note to another.

Kwa'ngwa mana called to her, signaling to follow her into the storeroom. *"I thought this would be a good time to show you the rest of our home. This is where Joseph grew up, as have many generations of our family."*

The storeroom which is an adjunct of their house was more than half as large as the dwelling. It was their insurance against a possible year of privation, their alternate for some of the public measures which have come about in the white man's world. Its value was reflected in their attitude of confidence, their self-sufficiently. She took Maya into the storeroom, and although a new harvest season would soon be here, it was even now well stocked. Ears of corn, sorted by color, were neatly corded – enough to carry them through and beyond a whole year of crop failure. Some of the corn was two or three years old. Bags of shelled beans, pieces of dried mutton strung on a wire, bunches of dried string beans, vines, pods and all – the supplies on hand were varied and plentiful. Later there would be watermelons available until January and squash throughout the winter.

Maya noticed curious dried spirals hung from three or four nails. These, she learned, were prepared from a young squash by removing the rind and cutting the meat in a long spiral, which was hung up in the bright sun to dry. *"But you must use a young squash, not an old one,"* cautioned Kwa'ngwa mana.

On another nail there was a big crook-neck gourd which was hollow and had a round opening in the shell where the stem began to enlarge to form the round body. It looked like something intended for nesting birds, but she set Maya right, *"We used to have those for carrying water,"* explained Kwa'ngwa mana. *"You carried it by the crook over your shoulder. When you made one you first cut the hole, then cooked the gourd, and cleaned out the inside."*

The older Hopi have retained some of the old Indian ways which others, especially the younger generations, no longer follow, customs which have no compelling significance and therefore yield to more convenient ways. Although there is a table in their living room, they usually prefer to eat from a mat placed on the floor. They would sit before this on other mats, preserving the postures which tradition had established. The woman would sit squarely, as though she had first kneeled and then sat back with her legs doubled beneath her. The man would sit with his left leg doubled under him, the right leg with knee elevated and foot squarely on the floor, a little advanced. *"Then, if anything happens and I need to protect my family, I can spring up quickly."* Hon'hoya had come back inside and demonstrated for her. He showed her how a girl or a young unmarried woman would sit on both hips but with her legs to one side, doubled at her knee and drawn in closely. That way, her skirt would cover her legs down to her feet.

Kwa'ngwa mana handed two five-gallon jugs to Hon'hoya, *"Take Maya down to the spring for water. We have much to do before our evening rituals. And when you return, Joseph should be here."* She saw a glow light up Maya's face in reaction. *"Yes, he is anxious to see you again. That's why he gave you the doll this afternoon."*

Maya wondered if there were any secrets at all in this household.

"Follow me," Hon'hoya led the way to the street, heading for the spring.

Maya knew to expect seeing many older men and women here, with dark wrinkled faces and gnarled hands. She found it interesting to listen to Hon'hoya's manner of speaking, rather gutturally, deep in his throat, and almost without moving his lips. Following this old man, she wondered what his age was. Perhaps eighty? Yet, he was so spry and moved so quickly. She was glad for his speaking English, for there was no white man who could master their language. Most Hopis learned English in school.

They were passing more older houses when she noticed another old man approaching, and he seemed yet older than Hon'hoya. *"Um pu ni'man?"* The man spoke so quietly to Hon'hoya, it was hard for Maya to hear his words. Then he seemed to notice Maya and said *"Hello"* in English, not to leave her out of the conversation. She became engrossed in watching the two older men talk. Although he carried a staff, the older man set it down as if saying he didn't really need it. Wiry and somewhat stooped, he walked with a springy step, as if living were an adventure. Short in stature, even for a Hopi, he was slender and seemed not to have an extra ounce of body weight anywhere. His face was brown leather, as brown as an old saddle. He had no teeth, except a few occasional flashes of yellowed stumps. Once possibly strong, his chin now was a continuous line from one jawline to the other – giving him a sort of *'Popeye'* face. His straight hair, falling almost to his shoulders, and worn without the usual bright bandeau, was almost white.

Hon'hoya needed to place his lips close to the old man's ear and talk at maximum volume. Whether hearing this or not, his failure made no difference in his responses. She found out later that he could hardly see, but he gave no indication. His eyes had the eager gleam of one who finds the surrounding world rewarding, however dim.

Along with an alert expression on his face, there was a

poise, an attitude of being at peace with the world, an expression that was the opposite of anxiety or frustration. Maya had seen the same expression on Joseph Pahana's face, in his pictures and on TV. And she would see it repeatedly on her visit here.

The Hopi do not forget that their mission is peace. And, as confidence and poise help to keep the physical body strong and responsive, a Hopi's physical fitness builds confidence and poise. That fitness determined the nature and extent of his activity, his age had no bearing on the matter. This was the ancient Hopi way. No matter what your age may be, no matter how old you were, you would always continue to do whatever you were able to do. This custom had been as fixed as the revolution of the earth.

Maya realized she was being introduced to this old man, and she smiled and gave a slight bow of her head in respect. She guessed his age at around a hundred years. It was obvious their talk had ended, and she bent to retrieve his staff for him, giving him a smile when she handed it to him. He smiled and started walking off again.

"That was my uncle, who is well over one hundred years of age," said Hon'hoya. *"I knew you would like him, all the girls do. He has his own garden near the spring which he tends each day."*

Maya had read so much about how the Indian lives to be quite old. But to actually meet not one but several already was to her amazing. She knew there was much more in store for her, and she was becoming eager to get at it. But she reminded herself, *'you don't hurry an Indian'*. They have their own speed and you must follow their lead. So, she relaxed and followed her guide, taking in the wonders of the mesa.

The spring was a half mile away. The path led across the broad, flat ledges of the top of the mesa. In occasional crevices, an isolated and red Indian paintbrush could be seen. In others, a prickly-pear cactus lay in wait with its spines. In some places, the smooth rock was covered with patches of lichen, bluish gray in the dry desert air. At one point, the trail crossed a broad, shallow depression, bordered at its lower margin by a few square yards of soil, held in place by a low stone wall, followed by other small areas similar in form. Here, if rain fell, moisture could be retained and beans could be raised. Step by step, the path slowly lost altitude, and as Maya looked back, she discovered that the houses of the village had disappeared over the rim of the world. On her right, across a great gulf, a distant prong of the mesa cut across the skyline.

Suddenly the trail dove down a rocky gully where a few stones had been moved into position to give some sort of footing. The descent here was steep, and so was the climb when you returned with your burden. Below this the path wound among big fragments of the mesa's face which had broken off and had lodged in confusion. A hundred feet beyond lay the spring, a broad pool, unprepossessing in the white man's view, but serving the village for nearly 300 years, and supplying the same community in its earlier site for several hundred more.

As they filled the containers, Maya asked Hon'hoya if all the villagers here had to come down for their water. *"No, some have trucks with large drums that they get their water from the windmill-pump storage tank, several miles away."* And he pointed for her. She couldn't see where he meant, but smiled as if she did.

During their upward climb back, carrying their 45 pounds each, he seemed to sense this type of activity was new to her, and to distract her from any pain she may be suffering, he talked about the village and agriculture here.

It seemed that on the farther side of the village, a hundred yards beyond the last row of dwellings, the mesa feel away in great vertical cliffs. At one place enormous fragments as big as a house had been dislodged and lay upon one another in great confusion. Standing on the mesa rim, you could look down on a region that seemed merely rolling but was actually made up of ridges and valleys, sandy plains and bordering hills. Small, irregular fields were scattered in the midst of these. Where sand had accumulated in slopes and dunes, peach trees were growing, their roots far down in soil protected from drought by the overlying sand cover, which also lay ready to drink up and hold whatever rain may fall. Paths threaded their way through all of this, along with occasional wagon tracks, for a pickup truck or team of mules.

Still further away, three or four miles distant, lay other fields where there was moisture beneath the surface of the ground. Down there below the mesa were the crop lands, available for use through the workings of the clan allotment system. With the first warm weather of spring, you would descend one of the steep trails, carrying on your shoulder the ancient Hopi version of a hoe, a formidable, handmade implement with a blade as broad as your two hands and weighting many pounds. Week by week, as the season moved along, the trip was made. There was much to do each day – preparation of the ground, planting, cultivation, more planting, more cultivation – corn, beans, melon, squash – erection of little brush windbreaks to keep the young plants from being covered by sand and smothered, removal of windblown sands from those which were buried in spite of brush. Down the trail in the early morning, when the eastern horizon began to glow with the first light of dawn, back to the top of the mesa when the sun had entered the '*house of night*' and was about to '*close the door*'. This was continued while the crops were making their start, until finally they were safely established. Only then could they spend a day now and then attending a ceremony or visiting other villages.

With the coming of harvest, more trips were made from the mesa rim to the fields down below. Loads of corn, squash and melons, to be stored away against the needs of fall and winter, were carried on their backs.

You could see other plots of cultivated lands along the road two or three miles from the village, only a few used as the region was too sandy and dry for growing. And there was an outcropping of coal beyond the village, to be removed by shoveling. There were supposedly millions of tons along the Black Mesa, going back to prehistoric times that had been used for heating primitive homes in this region.

Maya could feel the history here, as if she had stepped on another planet, looking at this old village, realizing how full their days were. It sounded like crowded days, but when you consider their slower, more relaxed pace, you feel amazed at how old their ways still were.

Maya stopped. She heard voices, much like at the shrines near the Cultural Center. When she told Hon'hoya, his face showed excitement as he pointed to a place nearby. *"That is where some of our ancestors were buried. You hear their whispers, just as you heard their thoughts at the shrines. You are blessed with a special ability. We must tell Joseph when we return."* But Maya wasn't sure whether she liked hearing these voices or not. The hairs on the back of her neck were standing up, as were the hairs on her arms. And she felt cold. She tried to shake it off as they continued back on the dusty street but kept thinking that it was a really creepy feeling.

She heard children's voices singing lustily, coming from behind her, in the direction of the trail that led to the spring. She turned around and saw two small girls, riding on a real burro which also carried a five-gallon can of water on each side. And almost immediately, they passed another *'concert'*. This one came from the interior of a homemade shelter in the open space back of a house, in a framework that could have been discarded from the body of a truck, covered sketchily with odds and ends of old blankets and canvas.

Maya found the sight and sound of these children was bringing back memories of her small son. Instead of happiness, she began feeling a deep sadness, and was relieved when they finally reached Joseph's house. She wondered if he was there and felt her heart flutter in anticipation as she carried her too-heavy

91

water jug into the house. Her eyes hadn't adjusted to the darkness within when she heard her name being said aloud in a deep, resonant baritone, bringing a blush to her cheeks.

CHAPTER 13

HOOVER BUILDING

Joel Wattenberg had left the conference room in the Hoover Building shortly after Tanner. F.B.I. agents Niehardt and Weatherford were left sitting, a little dazed, and very curious.

"What the hell is this all about?" Niehardt asked out loud, fully aware that his partner was probably thinking that same question. *"That guy's a real dirtbag character. And for some reason, he thinks he's above the law. That was obvious!"*

"Yeah," Weatherford added as he shook himself out of deep thought. *"The kind that feels any concern he has is a calling beyond any law. I hate to think he's getting us mixed up in anything like that,"* as he looked at his partner. *"You know, like something illegal."*

Niehardt laughed, as if his somewhat naïve partner had just cracked a joke. *"Well, what would we do, Petie, say no? Jesus, grow up, will you? Let's read."* He opened both files, setting them side by side on the conference room table so they both could read at the same time.

Ten minutes later, they each wished they had the option to say no. Weatherford still felt confused a little, *"I don't get it."*

"Get what?"

"This whole thing."

"Well then. Let me explain the highlights to you – Man named Pahana, Indian Chief, have big dream – he make-um famous, run for Big Chief of White Man's country. Sidekick is Tonto – he watch-um out for Chief. When Chief win, he hold big

pow-wow and take-um land from white man, give-um back to all Redskins. We find-um way to keep Indian Chief out of Big White House. We heroes. Live-um happily ever after."

"Damn you, Niehardt. I bet you were one of those nasty Nazis during Hitler's war in your other life. You're real bad news." Then, he couldn't help but smile; even though he didn't like the way his partner made fun of people, he had to admit it was kind of funny.

Niehardt smiled back, "Yeah, just call me Heinrich. What I can't understand myself is why these guys are taking this all so seriously. Give me a fuckin' break! Look at this handwritten note from the President, 'Gentlemen…we are not looking to make sense out of this – we're looking for the best way out of a national dilemma – a national emergency. We appreciate your help.' And then he signs it, as if he was our buddy or something. National emergency. I'd say that judgement's up for grabs, Prez."

"And look at this code crap, for Christ's sake, Ralph. We're really supposed to use these words, like call this Saxon-guy Tonto? Really? Is this guy for real, this Wattenberger? This code-crap is like they used in the first grade at military school. That's probably where this guy got it from – when he was a twelve-year-old cadet. What a freakin' joke this is."

"Well, I'll tell you Petie, I'm sure he doesn't give a rat's ass what we think. As a matter of fact, if he could hear us now, I bet he's have a firing squad ready for us in thirty seconds."

"Yeah, then some other lucky agents would get this plum assignment."

"Come on, partner. Let's pretend we're real agents. We've got a job to do."

CHAPTER 14

MISHONGONOVI

"It's you!" Maya blurted out. Then she felt her face redden as he laughed, announcing in his deep, musical voice. *"Yes, it is I."* Her eyes were becoming accustomed to the darker interior of the house and she noticed the scar below Joseph's left eye. It must have been covered up by makeup before, as she hadn't noticed it in any of his pictures.

"Joseph," Hon'hoya interrupted, *"she hears the voices too, like you do."* Putting down his water jug, he continued, *"At the shrines on the cliff near the burial place, she hears our ancestors. How can that be?"* He turned, looking more closely at Maya's face, *"Is she Hopi too?"*

Joseph smiled, reaching out for Maya's hand to take her out into the street, *"Let's take a walk."* Maya gave her water jug to Hon'hoya and kissed his cheek, saying she'd be back soon.

They talked a little as they walked to where her Jeep was, *"So, you hear the spirits."*

Maya looked at Joseph's profile, trying to read his thoughts, *"What does it mean? I am Sioux. Why do I hear the whispers of your Hopi ancestors?"*

"You are blessed. Very special insight that few have. Your kopavi is open. That is the 'open door' at the crown of your head," gesturing toward his own. *"It is where the spirits talk to you, and where our people used to communicate with one another in the first worlds. Not many know how to use it, or have the ability to do so."* They had reached the Jeep and he turned, looking deeply into her eyes, *"Amazing. Let's ride to the edge of the mesa and talk*

awhile."

She automatically gave him the keys and watched him handle the steering wheel. He appeared deep in thought, so they rode the short distance in silence. Through the still, silent air, Maya felt herself drawn to this stranger. There was a sense of power about him, an aura. It was very strong. She didn't know what it was, and she shifted in her seat, feeling uncomfortable, as she watched the edge of the mesa approach.

Joseph took her hand, picked up her doll which she had placed between the seats, and led her to a secluded spot to talk. They sat on rocks, looking at each other, not knowing quite where to start, when he leaned towards her, putting his hand on hers again, *"At last you have come. You have been expected, you know. When we know one another better, I'll tell you how I knew."*

He was looking closely at her, and she felt something jump inside. The eyes, the voice, the face, the way he tilted his head, the sudden arch of his brows, the easy way he moved his body. Old ways, disturbing ways, ways that draw you in. Ways that whisper to you in the final moment before you fall asleep, when the barriers have all fallen. Ways that rearrange the currents and space between male and female, regardless of species.

He touched the painted head feather on the doll, *"Did someone explain this to you?"*

Maya could feel her face blush again, thinking how ridiculous she must seem – a grown woman blushing like a young teenager.

"I realize there is much you want to know. We have a couple of hours before the final dances. I would like you to be there tonight – both in the plaza and then in the kiva. I will dance for you. Then we can watch the sunrise together and talk some more. So, Maya, what would you like to know first?"

"How do you know me? Do you really know who I am?"

Joseph laughed, *"Not very patient are you? And so curious. All right, it has been prophesized you would come."* He leaned closer, *"The spirits told me. And I had heard about you. Maya Chardon. Anthropologist. You helped pave my way in the trouble in the Black Hills years ago. It must have been interesting for you, meeting other Sioux Indians. Now that I have met you, I see how strong the Indian blood runs in you. I know you have been involved in many fights for the Native Americans. And I know that you and I are tied together in destiny. That is what I know."*

"What do you mean, tied together in destiny?"

His eyes looked into hers, *"You hold my future in your hands."*

Maya had to look away for a moment. His eyes were trying to look too deeply inside her. She wondered just how much he really did know. She took a deep breath, turning back and tried to fill in the gaps of information, *"My great, great, great grandmother was Sioux Indian, whose tribe was led by Black Rock, Ee-ah-sa-pa. My father was an Anthropologist, specializing in pre-Columbian civilization. I was named after his favorite, the Maya Civilization. My favorite has always been Native Americans. That's why I am here now. Well, partly why. I find you fascinating. Indian culture is an exotic flurry of metaphors – all of which makes for a transcendent way of life. But you, Joseph, are crossing over into the white man's world – a world of the credo 'What you see is what you get.' The typical white man craves evidence, logic, needing to see confirmation on CNN. It's difficult to appreciate the beauty of your complex society and your deep ties to the land and stars. How are you going to reach the white man, who is so afflicted with acute literalism?"*

"By speaking in terms he can identify with. Have you seen the talk shows I have done with Damon Sloane?" Maya told him she had only been able to read about the latest show. *"Then, you already know the answer to that question. I am simply asking*

people to change. And it has been customary in the white man's civilization to change everything that is natural. I am trying to reach them on a simple premise – look what you have done. Now, undo it."

"But you have also said it may be impossible to do that."

"Yes, I know I may not be able to reach all the people I need to. It seems an impossible task at best. But there are several million people who are changing. I have succeeded with them, at least."

"But don't you feel some hostility towards the white man – for trying to change you and your people?"

"Yes, I guess there is a part of me that does. Ever since the beginnings of community existence among the Hopis, some change must have been going on. But for centuries, change must have been too slow to even notice. Then came the real changes from the contact with the white man, the establishment of an agency, and the opening of a school to teach a new language and history. And now the hope of many whites is to mainstream Indians off the reservation into their white civilization. It wouldn't work, Maya. We are too different and self-sufficient. And the white civilization is too complicated. It moves too fast. It involves many things that are foreign to Indian experience and beyond his judgement. An Indian doesn't know how to effectively manage money. He is not ready for democratic government. He does not accept the decision of a majority and accept it as his own. Meanwhile, the Hopis stand as living representatives of an ancient way of life. We have not been touched gently by the transition that has begun."

Joseph Pahana looked out over the desert from their seats atop the Mesa. He stood up, taking a deep breath, holding out his arms as if to embrace the scene, *"Standing on a mesa so high, so* old, so revered is to be at the 'ceiling of the world.' Maya," he turned, looking down at her, *"the white civilization could very well kill this planet and everything and everyone on it. I have to try to stop it!"*

He sat back down, leaning toward her again, *"Change – always change. Always that which is different and better must be found. All of their progress – the white man points to his changes with pride. It's not a prideful thing sometimes, this change. Much of the time it is because of competition. In the white world, the man who is to make his mark must excel in his initiative and in the productive utilization of his talents. He must get ahead, which means that he must also get ahead of the other guy.*

"Our Hopi civilization is completely the opposite. We seek to work in harmony with the natural forces, great and small, not to harness them or to change them. Sometimes the white man in driving to get ahead is less than honest. Often he is far less than considerate. Because of this, a continuing price must be paid. At what price have the 'great material advances' been achieved? What is it that everybody wants?"

Joseph looked so frustrated. Maya knew he expected some kind of response from her. *"The 'white man' says he wants peace, but we are a nation that profits more in wartime. I can't figure it out either."* She reached over, placing her hand on his to show him she understood. She needed him to trust her, to open up to her completely. That was the only way to get her answers.

"We have been hurt in so many ways, Maya. Because of the outside interference from the white man, we are obligated to do things against our beliefs. Some of those who have been forced into conflict (war) have returned with such inner conflicts that they have turned to drugs or alcohol use. Our belief has always been that no man can indulge in anything that causes him to lose control of himself. We are concerned about our people.

Always, the negative impact on the Hopi world has come from outside interference."

Joseph put his other hand over Maya's, blinking away tears. She couldn't, feeling a few fall from her eyes. *"And yet, Joseph, you are trying to save these people. All these others who have hurt you and your people. Why?"*

"It is my purpose in being, Maya, to try to save this world. And anyone, regardless of color or race, who can be turned back from greed and immoral activities. Even if I fail, they still will be saved and can be included in the Chosen People, who will be saved when the world ends."

He looked up at the fading sun, *"I must go and prepare for the ritual. I have one question for you, Maya. Given a choice between the white man's complex world and our Hopi way, one that is relatively simple and basic, which one would you choose?"*

"I would choose your simpler life, with no hesitation. Why do you ask me that?"

He smiled and squeezed her hands, *"You will know soon. I will search for you after the rituals."*

She watched him walk back to the Jeep, feeling very deeply moved by their discussion. She couldn't be sure if he was simply a fanatic, believing everything he said; an aspiring politician who said what he was expected to and had to be an actor to achieve the right effect; or if he truly was the Pahana and all he said was really true. She hoped something would happen soon to tell her which one, because she was feeling herself falling under his spell. And she couldn't let that happen.

When they had returned to the house, Joseph disappeared quickly. Maya felt in the way, so she went back outside and sat on the wall, facing the mesa, where they had just been. She realized how little she really knew about the Hopi Indians.

"*A penny for your thoughts,*" a man's voice startled her. She turned and looked at an older man who seemed slightly familiar. "*I am I, Na'moki. I saw you at Kwa'ngwa mana's house.*"

Maya remembered. The medicine man. "*Please could you sit with me for a while?*"

"*Yes, I wanted a chance to meet and talk with you again.*"

"*I was just thinking how little I know about your people. Why didn't you feel you wanted a written language?*"

His old, lined face wrinkled more as he smiled, "*Ah, you are a curious one. When a religion such as ours is written down, it gets into unfriendly hands. A man who does not understand reads it and criticizes it. He says it is wrong, because there is no one to explain and help him understand. Another comes along and changes something, which is different from what it was intended to be. Then someone else reads it, says it's wrong and more changes are made. Then they will all argue over it. Each one thinks he's right and all others are wrong.*

"*We believe that is what has happened all over the world. It sets people against one another. Their religion doesn't help them the way it should. It makes them unhappy and they fight about it. With the Hopi, the rules and beliefs are spoken, not written down. An older man gives the instructions to a younger man, telling him the Hopi truths, just as he had been told before. The rule has been to learn them exactly, not to make any mistakes, never to forget them. When older, the young man will then tell his son or grandson. That is the way it has been with the Hopis for hundreds of years. We think it is the better way.*"

Maya asked him if there had ever been reactions within the Hopi people, against this strict, inflexible way in which they lived.

"Yes, we are human beings with human faults and weaknesses. Sometimes an individual, too ready with suspicions, has turned against others who were entitled to be his friends, resulting at times in self-induced fears and harmful concepts. But overall we are a remarkable people, aren't we?" His almost toothless smile was contagious.

Maya found this man, as she had found other Hopi, to be friendly and warm. She had been warned at the Cultural Center not to ask too many questions – that they would think she was an interfering, nosey outsider. But she had found these people to be open and interestingly frank, perhaps because of Joseph. As Na'moki was a medicine man, she was curious and asked him about his beliefs about the human body and its functions medically according to their traditions.

"I can only tell you my medical potion secrets if you were my son," again his irresistible smile. *"The living body of man and the living body of the earth were constructed in the same way. Through each runs an axis, man's axis being the backbone, the vertebral column, which controls the equilibrium of his movements and his functions. Along this axis are several vibratory centers which echo the primordial sound of life throughout the universe or sounds a warning if anything was wrong. The centers are here,"* he pointed to the top of his head, a spot between his eyes, his throat, his heart, and his navel.

Pointing to Maya's top of her head, he explained, *"The first of these centers in man lay at the top of your head, the soft spot at birth, Kopavi, or the 'open door' through which man received his life and communicated with his Creator. The soft spot hardened and the door was closed during man's life, until his death, opening then for his life to depart as it had come."*

Maya recalled how other religions postulated a similar series of centers of force and psychophysical centers in the human body. Eastern mysticism called the crown of the head the Sahasrara-Padma, the Thousand-Petaled Locust, associated with the pituitary gland of the brain. As with the Hopi, it was the *'door to the Creator'*, through which consciousness entered and left.

Na'moki continued explaining the other spots, the brain, the throat (as she had learned in her studies, the Visuddha Cakra), and the heart, which is *"a vibratory organ, pulsing with the vibration of life itself. When a man feels the good of life is of 'One Heart'. But those who permitted evil feelings to enter are said to be of 'Two Hearts'."* When Na'moki touched his own belly, *"People now call this the 'solar plexus', the throne in man of the Creator himself. From it, he directed all the functions of man."*

There were two more centers in Eastern mysticism that are not included in the Hopi series, the Muladhara Cakra, and the Svadhisthana Cakra. She also knew that the four lower centers represented successively the four elements that comprise man's body – earth, water, fire and air. Maya was pleased to see that both Eastern and Hopi mysticism equated the bodies of man and the earth, and the centers within man with the seven universes.

She asked him if he still cared for the sick. *"Yes, although many will go to the medical clinic if I advise. I also help the Navajo, though they wouldn't want you to talk about that."* He laughed at what must be an inside joke to them. Then he made a serious face, *"You know the First People knew no sickness, in the body or in the head. Not until evil entered the world. It was then that a medicine man could tell what was wrong with a person by examining the centers."*

He looked around, taking note of the activities and felt it was time to go. *"I'll take you back in to Kwa'ngawa mana and I shall get ready for my dance. I look forward to our next talk."*

Maya was feeling embraced by this Hopi history. These people were so committed to it – it basically dictated their lives. There seemed to be a very fine line between their spiritual world (who they were) and their physical world (what they were). She had never met any people like them – and felt she probably never would again.

CHAPTER 15

UNDER THE STARS

Maya sat on a concrete block next to Kwa'ngwa mana. They were waiting for the dancers to come out for the evening ritual for the public. There were about two hundred people squeezed into the plaza and on the flat roofs of the surrounding houses. She guessed it to be around six o'clock in the evening and noticed how brilliant gold the desert looked. There were teenagers wearing Apache Nation jackets, shawl-wrapped Hopi grandmothers, Navajo in Harley-Davidson t-shirts, and the usual children everywhere. The women with infants were back at their posts in the doorways of the houses. This was also the first dance that this year's brides were permitted to attend. Attired in their wedding robes, they stood demurely in the crowd. There was a hush that had settled over the crowd, and all eyes turned to the passageway where the kachina dancers usually entered.

The procession of the '*spirits*' began and the song and dance started with renewed vigor. Once again the kachinas were sprinkled with water and cornmeal. Then the leader of the Powamu-manas passed slowly along the line of kachinas and with an almost imperceptible motion raised her arm beneath her red and white cape in front of each kachina. It was a significant movement seldom seen, for underneath her arm and concealed by her cape was a pahosovi, a '*spiritual crown*' made of wood, round in form, painted and decorated. By lifting it up and down in front of each kachina, the Powamu-mana now made the same motion with a hoop in front of each child initiated into Powamu,, signifying purification of his '*Road of Life*'. The Kachina Father then delivered his farewell to the kachinas, *"Take our message to the Four Corners of the world, that all life may receive renewal by having moisture. May you go on your way with happy hearts and grateful thoughts."* After the leader of the kachinas shook his rattle, signifying acceptance of the message, it was over.

Villagers and Indians from other pueblos came up to pluck twigs of spruce from the kachinas to carry home and plant in their own fields. With the setting sun, the kachinas filed silently out of the plaza and through the narrow streets of the village, leaving behind a solemn silence. No man followed them, as they then descended to the Kachina House on the ledge below. Then they vanished.

Joseph Pahana left the Kachina House after removing his mask and washing his body of the paint, searching for Maya in the plaza. Then they went to a friend's house, a small house on the cap rock near the very tip of the mesa. They enjoyed mutton-and-hominy stew, meatloaf, fry-bread, crisp blue piki, roasted corn, roasted peppers, three types of beans and pumpkin pie.

As Maya sat back, feeling very satisfied, she noticed that this house was different in some ways, but still typical of many Hopi houses of today, especially those built in the last thirty or forty years. Though built of stone and with two rooms, the living room was larger. The walls and ceilings were plastered and the floors were made of matched boards. Also, the windows were larger and there were more of them. There were more material aspects in the furniture, reflecting a desire for greater comfort.

The owners of the house, Dan and Emily, showed more white customs, dressed as white people did, and even Dan's hair was like white custom, no Indian bobo nor bright bandeau. But their lives were filled as the other Hopi were, with his crops to attend to and she was skilled at basketry and cooked as the other Hopi women did.

Dan approached Maya, talking about the Hopi traditions for a few minutes. Then he said, *"We don't really ask you to understand our ways, Maya, which are so different from yours. But we do ask that you grant us the respect to live the way we want and need to, and not to discount our beliefs. Ever since the white* race made contact with us, they have put pressures on us. Some was necessary, I can see, because we must live together; which means we, the smaller, must adapt to you, the larger. But many have approached us looking upon us as inferior, telling us that there are better ways in store for us. These inflict scars that never quite disappear." Dan stopped, fearing he had been somewhat disrespectful to his guest.

Before the moment could be lost, Maya felt she had to be honest with this man, who had welcomed her so warmly into his home "I understand, Dan. You see, my ancestry is pretty much gone – and it makes me sad. I wish I could go to an Indian village where some of my family lived and visit them. Sometimes, I feel quite lost in the white man's world. My father felt that way too. That's why he preferred to live in a small Mayan village. He felt they were his people, living a simpler, more meaningful life. As I look around you and your village, I envy you. And I wish I could be more like you."

Maya turned to Joseph, "I want to know so much more. I need to know about your ceremonies. So many in the white man's world say Indian ceremonies border on the sixth-sense realm of mysticism. They dismiss them as crude folklore and erotic practices of primitives that have no relationship to the enlightened tenets of modern civilization. But I think that in becoming 'modern', we have forgotten our spiritual side. I want to be able to feel what you feel, at least in part. Can you help me understand, even a little of it?"

Joseph smiled and promised to tell her more. His mother also smiled at Maya, "You are beginning to feel it. You are finding your spiritual soul, Maya. To continue this journey, you must return to us some day soon. Or you will lose it again."

"Yes, I want to come back. I hope I will…"

"No, you must say, deep in your heart – you WILL return. You must, to find your peace. All mankind searches for inner *peace – but so many never have the chance to find it,"* she looked towards her son, *"and I worry when I see the danger of someone losing it."*

Maya saw the way Kwa'ngwa mana looked towards her son who was leaving the house, but didn't understand why. *"I see trouble in my son. His life is out of harmony. Maya, you are the one who can help him. I see that. He is outside. He always stands on an overlook when he needs to think, when he's troubled. Find him and talk with him. Please."*

Maya found Joseph outside, looking up at the stars. *"I'd like to tell you a story, Maya. A young Indian couple, Deer Hunter and White Corn Maiden fell so in love that they neglected their religious traditions. The people in the pueblo feared that the angry gods would send a disaster to their village, and eventually the spirits did exact punishment. The couple was shot into the sky and turned into stars, destined forever to chase each other across the sky."*

He turned and looked at her, *"Strong love can sometimes blind a couple. They should remember what their individual roles are and cherish their Creator as they cherish each other."*

They stood side by side overlooking the darkened valley. *"I look at you and think that you are one of us, not a Bahana. I see the way you are with my people, and how patient and caring you seem. You are a true Indian inside. You have touched me in here..."* He motioned to his heart.

Then he looked away to the valley below, *"As you can tell from some of the discussions you've had with us, that in all phases of our Indian culture, nature is treated as a sensitive entity with emotions of like, grief, and joy. The Indian's bond with earth is so profound that violating it is almost like betraying a family member.*

"As I travel around the country, in my message of peace,

our concern with helping to preserve the inherent harmony of the universal constituents of all life, reaffirms in all of us everywhere man's imperishable belief in the fullness and richness of life granted him by his creative forces, if he can just find a way of self-fulfillment."

"Joseph, I see all of that here. I can hear what you all say, I can even feel it. But, you step out there," Maya pointed off into the horizon, *"and it changes."*

"No, not really. We may sound like a very naïve people, living in the past, not facing today's more modern realities. But our mission is similar to the Road of Nirvana as conceived by Gautama over 2,000 years ago – right speech, conduct, aims, effort and state of mind. It even coincides with the 'Ten Commandments'."

"May I play devil's advocate for a moment, Joseph?"

He smiled, *"Go ahead."*

"You've studied American history and history of the world, for that matter. There have been many religious leaders that have come and gone. Many have destroyed peoples' lives by brainwashing them – telling them that they had lived a lie all their lives and they must atone for it by – well, by perhaps living without many material things, handing over all of their money, turning their backs on their families, etc. So many have proven to be false prophets. You seem to firmly believe in your role in our universe – to save our souls and save this world. Do you really believe all of that?"

Joseph stepped closer, taking her face in his hands, leaning very close, looking into her eyes. She thought he was going to kiss her. But he didn't. He instead said, *"Yes, Maya. I believe that is my role in this world. I believe it with all my heart and soul."*

Maya didn't dare breathe. His intensity and his closeness

was doing something to her. She had to think of something fast and snap out of it. *"What about temptation, Joseph?"* She was speaking so quietly, she was almost whispering. *"What if you find yourself facing temptation?"*

He stepped back, standing with his arms at his sides, turned and found them seats on a ledge. Sitting down, looking out over the desert, he waited for her to sit near him. She wondered why he was taking so long to answer her. Perhaps she had struck a nerve?

At last, he responded, but kept looking out at the horizon. *"Yes, there is always temptation. Just like Adam and Eve and their apple. I face it every day. And I overcome it. Or, I use it – to accomplish an end."*

"What do you mean, use it?"

"If someone came to me and said they needed me to help them. And at the same time, it would help me reach more people. Then I would say yes – and use them, while they used me. And we would both benefit."

He was going to tell her something significant. *"What do you mean, Joseph?"* she asked quietly.

He didn't answer, but kept staring out over the valley.

"Joseph?"

"Nothing, really."

She knew differently. She knew how to read people – and he was holding back. But she had to be careful not to push him too hard. She'd never find out anything if she did that. She'd have to bide her time. At least now she knew he appeared to be hiding something. She sat, watching him and waiting for him to break the silence.

"You know, Maya, there have been changes here – but yet

not. Our ancestral experience of living off the land has left its imprint on us today. But necessity no longer is the same – at least to the same extent. But many of the old resources haven't been forgotten, and our attitude of self-containment still persists."

He sounded as if he were rambling. She'd have to be patient and see where he was going with this.

"In remote times," he continued, talking quietly, as if there were no one around to listen, *"before there were any cultivated crops of consequence, or any domestic animals, a family was obligated to use what it could find or could devise, it if was to survive.*

"Today, we go to a trader for some things, a woman's dress, men's clothes and boots, even a pickup truck. But we still base our economy to a considerable degree on native resources. Building materials for our homes still come from the surrounding desert. We may have a few manufactured pieces of furniture, but they are basic and functional, like a table and chairs.

"The essentials for our crafts are here in the desert. Clay for pottery, fuel for fires, yucca for binder and galleta grass for filler in our baskets. Our men do the weaving of cloth, did you know that?" at last he turned and seemed to acknowledge her presence, smiling. *"We make our own looms and materials. But we don't grow our cotton anymore. I don't know how. I should, but I never learned weaving."*

He looked at her as if he wanted her to say it was all right. She wondered if he realized what he was saying to her, or where he was leading to. He looked almost as if he were in a trance. Functioning but not truly aware.

Joseph sat quietly smiling at her. *"I made your doll. I thought I had forgotten how – but I remembered. I made it for you."*

"Thank you, Joseph. I really like it. I'll cherish it forever."

Maya noticed his eyes had a weird look to them. She decided to try to bring him back to reality, hoping she wasn't talking to some sort of madman. But, before she could say anything, he put his hands over his face.

"God, that always happens to me at these ceremonies," he removed his hands and smiled at her, with eyes more alert. *"When we dance in these rituals, we become more than the man we are. It's like we become inhabited by a spirit. You'll see at the ceremony tonight. You'll feel it. The spirit invades us, all of us. You may even have an experience. Then you would understand.*

"These ceremonies give us such strength. You'll feel the strength too. If we weren't going to be in the kiva at sunrise, I would be standing here, praying. Stand up, Maya."

She stood up, and he turned her body to face the east, as he explained, *"Lesson one – face the east before light. You must be silent and worshipful while watching dawn's light appear. Your prayer would be called kuyiva'to."*

She stood quietly, only too aware that he was close behind her, so close that if she were to lean back in the slightest, her entire body would be touching his.

He whispered in her ear, *"It is time for kiva. Maya, I need you to stay with me. There is so much we need to know about each other. And you help me think, help me keep a clear mind about things. We must spend the next several weeks together. Come with me as I travel and speak to Americans. Can you commit that time to me? Is your need to know me as strong as mine to know you?"*

She wanted to lean back and feel his warmth against her. Instead, she took a step forward, turned around and faced him from some distance, so she could be objective.

"Yes, I need to know so much more about you, and your people. I have a sabbatical arrangement with the museum."

"We leave tomorrow, then. That will be a travel day, as I have a speech in California the next day. Can you be ready by mid afternoon?"

"Yes."

He took her hand and led her away from the edge of the mesa to the kiva, leaving her with just a squeeze of her hand, into the crowd that was gathering on the roof of the kiva. Someone gave her a folding chair to carry and use. She peered down into the kiva's smokey opening, looking at a fifteen-foot ladder that led downward. A man appeared with a lantern and motioned for her to enter. Rung by rung, she descended.

CHAPTER 16

THE KIVA

A whitewashed room with log beams, a concrete floor, and a pot-bellied woodstove at its center, the kiva measured about fifteen feet by thirty feet. On one end was a stone bench, on the other a raised platform where a group of old people (who had entered via the kiva's side door) sat in folding chairs. Maya sat along the south wall. The room was starkly lit by a string of bare yellow bulbs. In the glare, all eyes appeared sunken. It was as if people were already receiving messages from the *'other side of things'*.

When about forty bodies had jammed themselves into the kiva, an eerie falsetto yell floated down from above. The call came again. Then accompanied by stamping and the warning hiss of a gourd-rattle, several kachinas, repainted and masked, descended into the kiva. Several kachinas began to hum and dance around the kiva. Everything about them breathed power. And everything about them called up dark and thrilling images to Maya from her youth, before her vision had become constricted by abstraction.

All but four kachinas stepped away from the kiva center. These were the four leading chiefs, Naloonangmomwit. They carried out the important religious ceremonies from mid-winter to mid-summer. They took their positions. Eototo Kachina, who represented the Bear Clan, stood at the west, because the Bear Clan migrated from the west. The Parrot Clan leader stood to the south, as his clan migrated from that direction. He wore the ceremonial red and white cape of his sister, representing the female polarity. Since coming from the east, the Eagle Clan leader stood to the east. And at the north stood the Badger Clan leader. The kiva symbolized the body of the universe, and this cross-shaped ritual symbolized the *'Emergence'* and migration of the people and the spiritual uplift of man.

The Powamu Chief, standing near the side entrance, threw a sprinkle of water towards the Bear Clan leader, reaching forward with his hand, then pulling it back. He repeated that three more times, doing the same with the other leaders. The final time he took the thorny branch from Eototo's hands, swung it in a circle above his head, while walking around the kiva four times, indicating the raising of man's consciousness to the highest level. After repeating this ritual with each of the other leaders, the Powamu Chief left the kiva with the branches in his arms and blew smoke in each of the four directions. Then he led the four kachina leaders out to the Kachina House where he completed the tangave (religious act) by scraping their masks below the left eye. The kachina clan chiefs then each sacrificed an eagle on the housetop platform, to then quietly pluck the feathers and bury the bodies in ground west of the village in shrines of rocks, with sticks and pahos. This symbolized the spirits' return home.

Maya had fallen into a dazed half-sleep, waking to find herself looking into Joseph's face.

"It happened, didn't it, Maya? We lulled you into a trance."

"Either that, or I'm just tired," she answered with a yawn. *"Sorry."*

"You should get some sleep, we travel tomorrow."

Her Jeep drive back to the Cultural Center was short and Maya collapsed on the bed, still in her clothes. She wondered what kind of sleep she'd have. This had been a rather strange day for her. She wondered what had happened. Why did she become like a hypnotized person? She lay in bed, recalling visions of dancing feathers, dreamlike colors dancing. She felt the kachinas had been generous – but they hadn't made her a Hopi. She was an Indian – but an outsider here. And she had a job to do. She closed her eyes. Maybe not a trance, maybe just tiredness.

Maya didn't sleep well that night. Because of the children she had seen earlier that day, she kept dreaming of her son, as he was when he died – three years old, playful and innocent. After an hour of restless sleep, she found herself lying awake wondering what the significance was of her being at the usually-closed ceremonies that night? Her mind lingered over a question eternal, and always the same, *'Where is there any meaning in my life? Was she on the path that was chosen for her when her own life began?'* Maya felt as if she had been falling from the rim of a great, high place like these tall mesas, somewhere back in time, for all the years she had been living. And through all of those years, she has been falling towards something, or someone unsee. At the last moment before she again slept, she felt lost.

CHAPTER 17

REPORTING IN

Maya only slept a few hours but awoke feeling refreshed. She realized it was sunrise and rushed outside to enjoy the beautiful moment. It was early, before 6AM, but she was trying to readjust her mind away from the white man's clock to Hopi time, where they simply use the position of the sun. The approach of dawn, or *'white dawn'*, was kucha'nuptu. When colors began to surface soon after, it became sikya'nupty, or *'yellow dawn'*. As she watched the sun begin to appear, she thought the words, ta'wa ya'ma.

Maya looked toward the southeast across the Painted Desert, appreciating the misty, muted colors as they became more defined. Taking off her watch and putting it in her pocket, she thought of the Hopi words for the sky *'painted with light,'* tala'vaiyi.

Soon, she knew it was time to tear herself away from such a serene setting and returned to her room to pack. She decided she had better call Tanner. She looked forward to waking him up. It had been years since she had called him so early in the morning. It must be about 3AM there.

But he was still up, probably working quietly at home. *"Well, well, Pumpkin. How goes the investigation?"*

"Before I tell you, did you get my package yet? The one on the history of the Hopi?"

"Yeah. I read it a couple of times."

"What? Wasn't it what you wanted?"

"Near enough."

"Tanner, didn't you like it?"

"Well, it sort of told me something about you."

"What was that?"

He laughed, *"That you're smart, of course. I already knew that."*

She laughed too. *"Tanner, sometimes I really don't know what to think about you."*

"So, talk to me. Tell me something progressive and hopeful."

"Okay, first, these are wonderful, mystical people. I feel like I've walked back into history here. Even the more modern Hopi still honor their traditions…"

He interrupted her, *"No, Maya. Tell me about Joseph Pahana. What did his mother say?"*

"That he was born with signs that he was a spiritual person. Physical signs. And I don't mean his lighter skin and wavy hair. He has scars that he was born with, that are symbolic of some kind of eagle testing. He has one under his left eye and one on each side of his front torso."

"Did you, uh, check them out yourself?"

"Jesus, Tanner. Cut it out!"

"Well, I know what a babe you are. At least I recognize you as one. The guy's gotta be blind not to be turned on by you. Hasn't he made any moves on you yet?"

Maya didn't answer. Something just occurred to her.

"Maya, hello?"

"I'm here, Tanner. Damn you, how did you know?"

"So, he did come onto you?"

"No Tanner. How did you know he was here on the reservation?"

"I see all…I know all."

"Come on, Tanner."

"Did you honestly think we'd leave this guy only in your capable hands? We've been having him followed the last couple of weeks, Maya. We're not pulling our guy off just because you're there now. Besides, how do you know this guy's not potentially dangerous?"

"All right. I know he is hiding something. But I really don't think I'm in any danger."

"Wait a minute…what do you mean, you know he's hiding something?"

"He let something slip last night. He told me that if someone came to him with a proposal that he help them, that he's consider it, if it meant he'd reach more of the people quicker. I think your suspicions may prove out. He may just be considering politics."

"Do you have any proof?"

"No, just a feeling. It seems to make sense."

"Proof, dear. We need hard proof."

"I know, I know. Listen, Tanner, something else. He knew I'd be here. The whole village knew I'd be here. You want to tell me how he knew that?"

"Hold on now. Do you mean, he's said he knows you're investigating him?"

"No, no. He says the spirits told him about me. He thinks I'm here as an Anthropologist. And he knows about my father. He may know about the F.B.I. too, although he doesn't seem to act like he does. Of course, I think acting is second nature to this man. Could we have a leak?"

"Hmm, maybe. Okay, here's how we'll move on this. Send all your notes to me marked 'Personal & Confidential', sealed and taped shut. If something happens big, hightail it straight over here to Washington, especially if it's hard proof. I'm pulling all the files and locking them up in my safe. And I guess I'll pull the tail on him. We'll kind of act like we're not doing it anymore, like we've lost interest in him, you know? Then be really careful. Watch your back, okay?"

"Yeah, okay. Look – you may not hear from me for a couple of weeks unless I find out something significant. I'm going on the road with him."

"Really?? Well, maybe that's even better. No word from you means no more interest in him. And you'll be with him, so no other tail needed. Sounds good."

"No problem with it then?"

"None." Then he laughed.

"What? What's so funny?"

"I'm trying to picture this rather sophisticated and together dude being with you for the next few weeks. He's gonna start getting 'puppy eyes.' You know that, Maya."

"I have to admit, he's said things like 'I touch him in his heart', and 'I hold his destiny in my hands', or some such thing. And he is a bit 'touchy feely' with me."

"Ha! I knew it! And I can bet I know what he wants you to touch and hold in your hands."

"Don't get me wrong, Tanner. I have the greatest respect for these people. And I respect this man."

"Yeah right. All I can say is, experienced or not, this guy'll have the hots for you damned soon. And I bet you're overdue in that department."

Maya hung up on him. That guy could be heartless and cruel sometimes, and this was one of them. She hated the way Tanner's morals seemed to dwell in the gutter.

Maya took a long, relaxing bath, followed by an even longer, relaxing breakfast. Being a born people-watcher, she didn't always mind having to eat alone. There were times when she actually enjoyed it.

She finished packing her bags and checked out. She might as well enjoy the next few weeks. She was still angry with Tanner. She didn't owe him anything. This would be for her. Even if Tanner told her to quit the case, she didn't think she could. There was something about these people, and something about Joseph Pahana that was tugging at her.

Joseph was waiting for Maya when she brought her bags to the Jeep, sitting behind the driver's wheel. *"Surprise! I thought we'd go to the airport together. John will meet us there. Is that all right?"*

"Who's John?"

"Oh, that's right. You haven't met him. John is my best friend and constant companion. He also acts like my protector, sort of watching out for me. He uses his white name, John Saxon. His Hopi name is Sakwaitiwa, which means 'Animals Sun in Green Pastures'."

Joseph became a short-tour guide. They drove by several more Hopi villages, stopping at Old Oraibi before moving on. They sat there in silence, on the mesa ledge, near this oldest town in America and absorbed the beauty as if they were never to see it again. *"Whenever I come home for a while, I need to charge up my batteries before moving on. I get such a rush of feeling, looking out at this land, that it fills me up. I try to make it stretch until I can come back."* Maya could feel his sadness as they sat there together.

The landscape in the distance revealed a panorama of colorful canyons and mesas. The haze floating on the horizon blended with the pastel shades of peach, pink and red with a distant blue-green mantle of desert vegetation, and spots of gray, slightly overcast sky, mingled with the bright blue. They were taking mental pictures of the creeks, darting through the mesa canyons, black in the shadows, silver in the sun.

Maya felt a serene peacefulness she had never known anywhere else, not to the depth she was now experiencing. The Mayan village had given her only a hint of this. It seemed so long ago, when she had been there just a few weeks before. The land here soothes and challenges. It is considered holy land by its occupants, the Hopi people. It is a place to see their visions.

CHAPTER 18

HOOVER BUILDING

There were times when Elliott Tanner hated his job. He had lied to Maya. Not a lot. Only a little. That didn't mean he liked having to do that. He planned to keep a couple of guys watching Maya and Joseph. He couldn't risk anything happening to her. And, Tanner felt really uncomfortable about Niehardt and Weatherford. Not because of them – they were good agents and did their jobs, no questions asked. But they were following Wattenberg's orders now. And Tanner didn't trust that guy.

He stared at the pile on his desk. He certainly couldn't lock up the files, either. Not with the President on their back, wanting all kinds of information on this guy Pahana. Well, maybe he lied a little to Maya, but it was for her own good.

Tanner's phone rang. The inside line. It was Director O'Toole. *"Elliott, better get in here. I think I've got something you need to see."*

F.B.I. Director O'Toole sat red-faced behind his desk, *"Close the door, Tanner. I've just discovered something that has been sitting on top of Main's desk for weeks."* Special Agent Richard Main had a heart attack a few weeks earlier and had just died.

O'Toole opened a very fat folder, taking out some photographs and audio tapes, laying them on his desk. He picked up each photo, looking at it before handing it to Tanner. *"Know who this is?"*

The first picture showed a man in hunting clothes, walking in front of a large log building, with a lot of woods around the building. The second photo was a closeup of his face. *"Yeah, Chief. This is David Gordon, the political strategist. He's best known for his appreciation of the adversarial relationships between high-powered officials and the high-profile journalists who covered them. As a matter of fact, he is supposed to be advising our current President on media relations."*

"Yup, that's him. These pictures were taken on a surveillance job that Main was in charge of." He reached over his desk to Tanner with more pictures. *"Now, look who was having a little tete-a-tete with Mr. Gordon at his retreat in the burbs of Chicago."*

"This one I recognize – can't remember his name right now, but he served as deputy attorney general a few years back. This one is a retired Army officer by the name of Barnes, with a background in defense communications. This guy I recognize as a former Justice Department official. These two guards look like C.I.A. men. Definitely not ours.

"And…what the…? What the hell is he doing there? Patty, this is Pinkerton. He was there?"

"Yes, it's Pinky, the Director of the C.I.A."

"I don't understand this at all. What does this mean?"

"Well, Main was on a special assignment, tracking Pinkerton. There was a strong feeling that he was setting up a conspiracy that would help the opposition get back into the White House. Several months ago, he was in a series of meetings with Gordon, even before Gordon began advising our current President. This file is hot, Elliott. Wait until you hear some of their conversation at this meeting. But before I play you the audio highlights, here's someone else that came to the weekend gathering." He handed Tanner another photo.

"Damn, Patty, this is Joseph Pahana."

"Yup. What we have here is positive proof of a Planning Committee to take over the White House next year. Let's listen to

the important portions of their weekend discussion. I've listened to all of the tapes and edited them down for this meeting. These are the voices you'll be hearing." He handed Tanner a listing of the men whose pictures he had just seen: Pinky, Gordon, Pahana, General Barnes, Glenn Paine, a budget-planning expert, and Ted Knowles, a media agent. It looked to Tanner like Joseph Pahana was already in, and the guy was meeting with his new administration.

Gordon's voice was the first one heard, *"We have much to discuss gentlemen. First, the campaign issues are, as usual, domestic policy and foreign policy. But before we get to that, let's address the problem of 'distrust of government.' People don't believe anything they hear from Washington anymore. Joseph, as planned, you have been out there making speeches about that, appealing to the individual American about recapturing his power of choice and control over his government. Our overall strategy is to get the public to trust you – feel like you're on their side. This is your schedule for the rest of this year. Then, next January, you officially announce your candidacy and revisit each area in the same order. You have already toured New Hampshire, Iowa, Vermont, Massachusetts and Florida. Next week you will tour Illinois, North Carolina and New York City. Then you wanted two weeks free to visit your family – something about a ceremony. Your agenda picks up in California at the annual convention series in Los Angeles and San Francisco. Then you will revisit Chicago, then travel to Wisconsin and Pennsylvania.*

"The rest of the year we will concentrate on Texas, Georgia, Indiana, D.C., Alabama, Nebraska, West Virginia, Maryland, Michigan, Oregon, Idaho, Nevada, Tennessee, Kentucky, Arkansas, Rhode Island, Montana and South Dakota, in that order. You will occasionally be revisiting California, New York and Ohio. These are our biggest primary states with the most delegates. Starting in January, after our announcement, your agenda will be a very concentrated tour of all of these primary states in the same order. Your agenda is in the same order as the

primary voting. January in Iowa, February in New Hampshire, and so on. By the time the convention takes place in August, next year, you should be the only man we have left holding the flag.

"And, because your time will be spent basically campaigning, we have to discuss the basic issues now – so you'll be ready with proper answers in case someone anticipates our plans. Now, let's talk domestic issues."

O'Toole stopped the tape, and leaned over toward Tanner, *"They pretty much talk a lot of domestic bunk. I've taken out a lot but left in some interesting comments. The next voice you hear will be Glenn Paine, reading supportive stats on the domestic front…"* He started the tape up.

"All right, let's say you are asked to comment on 'What is wrong in America today?' You would respond, 'There is an increase in single-parent families, up 1,100% over the past three decades. Is this how we value love?' And then you add these stats, 'The wage and salary structure of American business, encouraged by federal tax policies, is pushing the nation toward a two-class society. The top 4% of the workers, which are 3.8 million individuals and families, earned $452 billion in wages and salaries – the same as the bottom 51% of workers, 49.2 million individuals and families. The 'middle class' is being dismantled. The decade increase of 2,184% in total salaries of people earning more than $1 million overwhelms the measely 44% decade increase in total salaries of people earning $20,000 to $50,000.'"

Gordon interrupted, *"Yes, that is excellent. Everyone can relate to those figures. Then you could go into something like this, 'Ask yourself if you have worried…*

- *that you are falling behind, not living as you once did.*
- *that you are going to have to work extra hours, or take a second job, just to meet your bills.*
- *that the company you have worked for all these years may dump you for a younger person.*

-   *or that the pension you have been promised may not be there when you retire.*
-   *that you are paying more than your fair share of taxes.*
-   *that the people who represent you in Congress are taking care of themselves and their friends at your expense.*

"*And as they are all nodding in agreement, you continue with, 'Sound familiar? The already rich are richer than ever. There has been an explosion in overnight new rich. Life for the working class is deteriorating and those at the bottom are trapped. For the first time, we are in an age where it will be impossible to achieve a better lifestyle than our parents. Most of us will be unable even to match our parents' middle-class status. Indeed, the growth of the middle-class, one of the underpinnings of democracy in this country, has been reversed….by government action.'*

"*You see, Joseph, you need to say things that everyone can identify with. And add, 'Understand too, that barring some unexpected intervention by the federal government, the worst is yet to come. For we are in the midst of the largest transfer from the middle-class to the rich, and from the middle-class to the poor, courtesy of the people in Washington who rewrote the rules.'*"

O'Toole stopped the tape, "*The rest of this side is discussion of domestic issues and comments that Pahana and Gordon read out loud.*"

The tape continued with Joseph Pahana's voice reading, "*For a great many Americans, Washington no longer seems to work. Like Muslims bowing to Mecca, we keep turning to our capital with hopeful eyes, looking, if not for a miracle, at least for some improvement in our lot in life. We wonder – all that expense, all that calculation, all that exercise of the will – what has it come to?*

"*Sometimes in frustration at the failure of our government to solve our problems, we wonder if our country is perhaps run by a foreign power, that is speaking in an alien tongue, addicted to orgies of self-congratulation that we have no share in. Americans end up feeling like our politicians have transformed our governmental system into 'us' and 'them'. 'Us' is Americans, sprawled in bewilderment across a continent; 'them' is Washington, perpetual generator of useless intrusion and insatiable demand.*

"It wasn't always that way. For better or worse, Washington, D.C., rose from the ashes of the Revolution as our guiding Phoenix, a tattered bird of passage leading into the future, quintessential representative of the pioneer spirit.

"What went wrong? There are those who have attributed our malady to the decline of leaders who followed George Washington's footsteps. The springs of political virtue became increasingly sullied. When the politically-conscious Americans asked for a higher standard of excellence, it was too late. The gap between results and intentions was too wide and it strained the souls of Presidents who tried.

"Our government had become a structural enterprise with modes of belief and expectations far away from the moral, ethical code and common sense that our government started with. The power of politics had become isolated – a culture unto itself – unresponsive to the citizens of the country it shared."

You could hear rustling of papers, as Pahana didn't seem to like the comments he had read, and paused, *"Whoa – don't you think this is all too strong and critical? I want to get elected, but I don't believe I should cast such large stones. Why not just stick to the facts – the results of a very incompetent group of leaders? All Americans can relate to that…"*

Gordon replied, *"Okay, no problem. We can rework these comments."*

O'Toole stopped the audio tape player for a moment, needing to stretch his arms and back, and loosen his neck muscles, *"Do you need anything Elliott? This is going to be a long listening session."*

Tanner took a deep breath, thinking this was not what he had planned to be working on today. This all definitely put a cap on Maya's assignment. She really needs to watch this guy even closer than thought. *"No, I guess I'm okay, Chief. Thanks. They sure know how to put together political speeches, don't they?"*

"It's called practice. Lots of practice. Ready to hear more?"

Tanner nodded, and they started listening again.

Gordon was talking again, continuing reading from the speeches, adding, *"Joseph, we can put in a lot of your own past comments here, and they'll work well."*

Over the next 45 minutes, Gordon read on about financial decline, sexual moral decline, new, incurable diseases, health insurance, how foreign countries are benefitting from trade agreements, and then about lobbyists who have clout. This is where Pahana interrupted, *"Isn't that going to anger the lobbyists we are courting to support us? Should we really talk about how they block tax-law changes that would be benefitting the few at the expense of the many?"*

Gordon replied, *"No, they expect to hear some of this. They know you are working hard for the public vote. No problem. We'll warn them ahead of time so they won't be surprised."*

Glenn came back into the conversation, *"You can also add to this about a capital gains tax cut, which is all nothing new. We've all heard it before. It calls attention to the fact that we need to learn all over again how to 'do good', and stop 'doing evil', right Joseph?"*

"Yeah, I guess." Joseph Pahana's voice reflected a less than enthusiastic attitude. Tanner secretly wondered if this is the first time that Joseph Pahana was realizing that he was going to

be pushed around by this group, possibly into doing things he may not always agree with. If he doesn't realize this now, then he is not as much of a genius as they all thought. He actually felt a little sorry for the guy.

O'Toole stopped the tape again. *"It starts getting more interesting, Elliott. General Barns talks next about their military program plans."* And started up the tape.

You could hear the General's stern voice, *"The military is definitely going to be a challenge. There are currently actions that continue downgrading the military in personnel, in importance. What we need to do basically is twofold: tell them we will put a freeze on military cutbacks, that the military is lean enough. Secondly, tell them the military is important to us.*

"One of the ways we will do that is rebuild the damage done during the Vietnam War. Rebuild the cohesion of a combat unit. We currently have a military that does NOT represent the variety of talents and points of view of the country as a whole. It's a military that has no connection with a significant part of the population – that part that produces the leaders of the rest of our institutions. The educated elite has a general ignorance of military affairs." The General then read about his planned five-part military program which would essentially add better educated people who are also generally wealthier to their military personnel, along with practices that would improve unit pride, use more training and restore morality and ethics and supposedly stretch the taxpayer's financial investment.

This time, Tanner reached over and stopped the tape. *"Wattenberg would love to get his hands on these tapes, Patty. I don't think it would be ethical to let him, do you?"*

"Damned right, Elliott. There's no way in hell I'm letting that asshole near this stuff. Let's hear the rest, the edited comments for Pahana to make on international relations. David Gordon is reading them here…"

Gordon read on about the problem, in his eyes that could lead to catastrophe, the diverse national and cultural groupings that make up the world's population which retain attitudes and habits left from a larger world when contrasting civilizations were far removed from one another. These grave difficulties can only be solved on a global scale. He went into detail about how computers can be used to produce '*correlation coefficients, charts and statistically expressed hypotheses.*' He suggested that instead of talking about solving the international dilemma, talk about a simple plan questioning the relations between races, between ethnic and religious communities, geographic groupings, to question the segregation of wealth from poverty and even men from women. He concluded, *"We have to say some generic promises that will please the public ears but not be too specific, and add some dramatic touches like, 'The current frustrations of contemporary life will only bring on a neurotic breakdown of our whole society. There is much to be said in the Eastern cultural tradition of balancing the yin-yang duality of our country's personality. Life does not usually permit a choice between problems. We will either survive by handling both our domestic and foreign problems with adequate skill or we will fail totally. And that would mean the end of our society and our world.'"*

O'Toole stopped the tape, *"Aren't you glad I edited this shit down? Now, Elliott, we happened to hear something that is probably going to shock you. It did me. It's pretty short and to the point."* He reached over and pushed the PLAY button.

They heard Joseph Pahana's voice, *"Gordon, a question. All of our work together has been most impressive. We have great speech ideas; we're putting together great plans and programs. But from all I've heard about the game of politics, it's very hard to unseat an incumbent President. Especially our current President, whose popularity is pretty good."*

Gordon's voice was fairly quiet, as if he wanted only Joseph to hear, *"Joseph, you're right. Generally, it's hard to unseat a popular President. But we have plans to take care of that. Leave that to us."*

Tanner, who had been leaning back in his chair, listening almost casually, sat up, looking extremely attentive all of a sudden. He turned up the volume.

Joseph reacted*, "What do you mean, taken care of?"*

Gordon responded even quieter than before, *"Well, let's just say that he won't be around to continue being a problem for us. Joseph, he may be popular with the voters, but he's in our way. So, we'll simply get him out of the way."*

"Jesus Christ!!" Tanner jumped up, rewinding the tape so he could hear that statement again. After he heard the same comment by Gordon, he stopped the tape. *"My God, Patty! Do you know what he's saying? There IS a conspiracy. I think they are really saying that they are going to do something to the President."* He sat back in his chair, wiping his forehead since he was sweating quite profusely from hearing Gordon's statement on tape. Then, he reached over the pushed the PLAY button for the rest of the tape to continue.

"Do you mean what I think you mean?" It was easy to hear a difference in Joseph Pahana's voice, as if he were very disturbed. His chair sounded like it was moving, like he was standing up.

"Now, Joseph, you're a smart man. What do you think? How badly do you want to be President? Well, we want you to be just as badly. And we're going to make sure. But timing is everything. And our man Pinkerton will handle it. Now, I suggest you leave everything to us. Relax. We'll be meeting with you again in a few weeks, in D.C."

O'Toole leaned over and stopped the tape. *"That's it. A conspiracy all right. And I'm putting our best men on it. We've got Pinkerton covered. I don't think they'll do anything until next year,* closer to the election. I sure can't see our Veep Corky running this country, can you? And, I know Pinky wouldn't want that either. But when the time's right, we'll be ready. Damned C.I.A.! They think they're Gods – each and every one of them!"

Tanner seemed to be in deep thought, reflecting on all he'd heard. *"We need to listen in when Pahana gets back here. Do I handle that? Or your men watching Pinkerton?"*

"You get a bug on Pahana, get Pumpkin to do it. Don't let her in on this unless she uncovers something and you have no choice. The less she knows the better."

"What about Wattenberg?"

"He'll know none of this – yet. All of this, tapes, papers, etc. gets locked up in our XGDS files, tabbed OP-COUP. I'll keep you informed, Tanner. I think we'd better talk every day on this."

"Jesus, Patty. Pinkerton right in the middle of this. If Wattenberg finds out, he'll have Pinky's head. What the downside of all of this – for our concealing it from the President?"

O'Toole cleared his throat and tried to sound relaxed, *"I think it's an even longer story, and I don't know all of it. I try to keep my distance from the C.I.A., believe me. I have enough to worry about. All I know is that there have been some illegal things Wattenberg has done. So he's no one to throw stones. If we wait long enough, these boys will both hang themselves. We just have to be ready to clean up the mess."*

Tanner pushed his chair back and walked over to the window. It was dark now, and the traffic was still slow and heavy. It was nice to have these mysteries revealed to him, but they created more mysteries. He just wanted to leave. He was tired of running and being chased, tired of wondering who did what and why, tired of sharing the guilt for these damned things. And now, he had put Maya right in the middle of it.

CHAPTER 19

ON THE ROAD

For the next few weeks, where Joseph Pahana went, Maya went. There was a lot of traveling and a lot of speeches. She seemed to spend more time with John Saxon than with Joseph. They usually booked a suite of rooms, sharing a common lounge area. She would hope to see Joseph there, but he always seemed to have meetings, or after-speech sessions with the press and others who wanted to talk with him. And then there were radio and television talk shows and guest appearances. She was wondering whether she might be wasting her time. She was learning nothing about his political aspirations nor his motives.

One afternoon, she decided to sit in the audience, rather than stay backstage. She wanted to see and feel what it was like. There were perhaps 700 people, packing an auditorium made to seat 500. She found a spot in the back of the room, in a far corner. She didn't want him to see her. As she looked around, she felt amazed that he seemed to draw these large crowds everywhere they had gone.

As he came out and began talking, she became caught up in what he was saying and doing. He had a portable microphone and moved down into the audience from the stage every so often. He appeared to want to be near the people – and they needed to be able to touch him. He was so handsome and charismatic, he made you feel he was indeed a prophet. She watched and listened to him.

Joseph stood on the stage, with one hand gesturing, *"E. L. Doctorow has said, 'We're living a national ideology that's invisible to us because we're inside.' Like a fish in the ocean cannot analyze the ocean. But there is a way. And each one of you need to do this.*

"I will be a witness to your change. And my responsibility is to show you how. Here is a little exercise which I now ask each of you to do. Close your eyes. Now, think of something that happened to you recently, or something that you read about that caused you to be glad. You were happy it happened, and the reason you were happy was – because it was the right thing. It was a good thing that happened. Consider it for a moment.

"I see a lot of smiles appearing. Some of you are even laughing to yourselves. That's good. Now, erase that memory for a moment as if you had written it on a blackboard. Now you will write another memory.

"This memory is sad, an unhappy remembrance – something you did, or someone did that brought pain, or that made you feel guilty or ashamed.

"I see those smiles disappearing. Now I want you to think to yourselves why this memory makes you unhappy. See the words as you think them. Answer this in your mind – was it a wrong thing to do? Yes, it was, wasn't it? And that is why you can't smile as you recall it. Now – take a few moments to mentally write on the blackboard three different ways this could have been handled differently. There are probably many things that could have been done – but think of three separate alternatives.

"All right. Now pick the one that would be the right thing to do. You can see it. The answer is clear – the right thing to do. Now picture the same situation again – only this time the right thing was done, and the results are transformed. Now I see some smiles again. Good.

"Because now you are transformed. You have become empowered with the wisdom of right and wrong, good and evil.

And you have seen the change. You have felt the change.

"Now, open your eyes. See how much better you feel now? I want you to do one thing in your lives from now on. And this is every minute of every day. Take each situation, think of the three alternatives you have, and pick the one that will make you smile and feel good about yourselves. That action will be the right thing to do. In every situation, from now on.

"Don't promise me you will do this. Promise yourselves. And now, go in peace…"

He left the stage. No matter how much they screamed for him, he never returned to the stage. He had done his part, and said what he wanted to.

Later, Joseph had a meeting to go to without John Saxon. So Maya and John went to the restaurant in their hotel and had coffee. Maya wanted to take advantage of this quiet time to pick the brain of this quiet, often brooding man.

"Is it difficult to be so far from the reservation so often, John?"

"Yes, it is. I don't like white people that much. So I miss my own kind." His eyes, dark and mysterious, seemed locked on hers. *"I carry my memories of my home with me. That helps a little."*

"If you miss the reservation, why are you doing so much traveling with Joseph?"

"I want to see Joseph be able to get us back what is rightly ours. Every morning Joseph says to me, 'Today, I will face in this world what is to be done that was told in the prophecy.'"

"So, you believe totally in Joseph and the prophecy?"

John looked at her as if she had asked something that should have been obvious. *"Joseph and the prophecy are our hope for the future. In 1882, Red Cloud said, 'The white man made us many promises, but he kept only one. He promised to take our land and he took it.' We only have a small portion left of the sacred land we once had. Our land IS our religion. All we have left is our religious tradition and our prophecies."*

"Strange. Religion was supposedly a strong part of the Spanish geographic expansion. I'm amazed they weren't more successful in forcing their religion on the Hopi people."

"About 2% of our people are converts to other religions. The Spanish brought Catholicism to the Indian people in 1680, but mostly in the New Mexico area. They built missions, gave the Indians Spanish names and made communicants of them. The Indians worship in those churches today, while still maintaining their own original ceremonies. The Hopi fully expected the Spanish to come to us and do the same. That's when we moved our villages to the top of the mesas from below, for defense. We don't have Spanish names, but we do have some Protestant and Catholic active missions.

"Inevitably, the missions in an Indian country are likely to develop narrow as well as broad views. Missionaries find it difficult to accept our beliefs and views. Literally, they close their minds to any sympathetic interpretation of what they see and hear, unable to understand.

"The Hopi people tolerate the missions on the reservation. The missionary has his own way of existence and like any other human being, is entitled to follow his own devices. No one should tell him what he ought or ought not to do. If he fails to understand Hopi beliefs, that is his misfortune but also his privilege. If he infringes on sacred Hopi rituals, he is harming himself, not the ritual which is too strong to suffer much harm in that way. If a Hopi has adopted the religion taught by a missionary, he simply attends their mission services. In other ways, he may seem no different from his neighbors. He may continue his interests in the ancient ceremonies, not as an active participant, but as an active spectator.

"As Hopis, we try to preserve what may be lost to us forever. If we begin to lack that sense of proportion, that endangers our 'Road of Life' with a false set of values. Even with the white man's scientific revelations, they find themselves scrambling along the brink of conflict. In their search for truth, they forget to search their past. All could be lost now – without their re-recognition of religion, and religion is the dependence on an entity better and larger than yourself.

"One of Joseph's businessmen was making fun of his prophecy. Joseph said nothing, except that the man simply didn't understand. Well, it made me angry. I shouldn't have said anything. But I couldn't help myself. Now, I am no longer welcome to go to his meetings."

"What did you say?"

"I guess I called the man a fool, and asked him, 'What makes you think your magic is real and ours isn't? Your prophets walked on water and parted the seas and raised the dead. And you say our prophets are bullshit? Our people have been practicing the same medicine for over 10,000 years. It's real and it's powerful.' And then I left, before I said any more. Later, Joseph told me that I couldn't go with him anymore. So, I see little of him now."

"That must be hard on you."

"It makes it hard to do my job. I am his protector from harm in the white man's world. The white man is a con man." It was easy to see the anger in John's eyes. *"Joseph is going to get our land back. That's the whole reason for this political charade. Their biggest con job yet is taking land away from the Indians. He's not at war with the enemies of the USA, but with the government of this country itself. Over something that took place over a hundred years ago. Time doesn't matter. Maya, nailing them does. They were all the God damned same, whether in their silly-frilly frock coats of a hundred years ago, or their pissy-elegant, tight-assed*

pinstripes of today. They have shit on our people and we will shit on them. I know you understand, you are Indian too."

Maya decided to take a chance, *"Do you mean, that if he does become President, he'll make sure that you get your land back?"*

The question didn't seem to surprise John. *"He has promised to get as much land back as possible for many Indian nations. Not just ours, but even yours. Do you really think that he was going to try to become President of the white man's country just to try and save more souls for the Fifth World?"*

"That's what I believed." She needed to act as if Joseph had told her his plans.

"Don't be so naïve, Maya. Joseph's involvement with these businessmen and their political world is not to get rich. Nor is it to make this country a paradise. That is the usual white man's reason. Riches don't make a man richer, just busier. And Paradise and Hell are both earthly places, inside each of us. We carry both of them inside us, wherever we go.

"Living in the white man's world has changed Joseph. When he first started as an attorney, he went too much by the book. And when the book didn't match the legal action, he kept looking for more books. It's not in the books! At least not the ones you can read. And he finally realized that. It's inside you. You know when something's right and when something's wrong. And, what the white man has done to the Indian is wrong. But we know that there's no way that the Supreme Court is going to give us back our land. If anything, they'll offer us money. Probably money that they don't even have. Just to pacify us."

"You know, John. You're talking more like a white man, angry and rebellious. Not like a peaceful Hopi."

Instead of becoming angry with Maya, he smiled. *"I know. What is the saying, 'When in Rome?' You know, no matter what we do, eventually it won't even matter."*

"What do you mean?"

"Because this world is almost over. The Emergence into the Fifth World has begun. You can read this in the earth itself. Plant forms from previous worlds are beginning to spring up as seeds. This could start a new study of botany if people were wise enough to read them. The same kind of seeds are being planted in the sky as stars. The same kind of seeds are being planted in our hearts. There is a plan, the plan of the universe and everyone in it. With the natural disasters' destruction, the new disease killing people by the thousands, millions, is there any doubt that the end is near? And now that Pahana is here – it will happen soon."

He rose ending the discussion, *"It's time to go."*

Maya followed John silently to the elevator. She felt sorry for him – he seemed torn between the painful present and the hopeful future of the new world. What if he was right? What if it didn't matter who they were or what they were trying to do? That this world couldn't be saved because it was already too late? If that's what John and Joseph really believed, then why were they fighting so hard to make this world better? None of this made any sense to her. Maybe they were confused too. Sure sounded like it.

As they reached their floor, there were two men getting on the elevator. And Maya recognized both of them. Both were the opposition party leaders and had served previous Presidents. Now that she knew Joseph was serious about running for political office, what should she do? How could she tell Tanner when she didn't have real proof and no details?

The suite lounge area was empty, and John went to join Joseph behind closed doors. Maya decided now was a good time to finish reading the brief for the Supreme Court case Hopi Nation VS U.S.A.

As she read through the 200-page brief, she mentally

compared it to his previous case writings. There was more of a commentary mixture than factual. Yes, he included proper dates, laws, treaties. But he made assumptions and they were fairly emotional. It read like a historical novel. To prove U.S. deceit and dishonesty, he referred to broken treaties and illegal laws. This was supported further by letters to Presidents and from Presidents. There was a copy of the Treaty of Guadaloupe Hidalgo that protected their land title deeds. He cited examples of what separate branches of the U.S. government seemed to work against one another through contradicting laws and opposing factions. The injustice was obvious when it was all put together like this.

To Maya, it read like a nightmare, because of who she was. An Indian. One law enacted recognizing Hopi rights to their land, and then the government ignoring their own law, because of gold being discovered in California and Hopi land was the quickest way to get there. In the government documents, the Hopi Nation was referred to as Moqui.

Overall, there was so much more supportive documents for the Indians than for the U.S. government. It made fascinating reading. She wasn't sure which were the hidden documents that were considered 'missing links' by the media. She didn't think it really mattered, sure that all she read was authentic.

Maya wondered what good all this work was going to do for the Hopi People. Starting all over again in their Fifth World may be the only solution. There was no way any white man was going to give up his land. Even if the Supreme Court said to. How could Joseph, as President, even do that? The white man's Congress would impeach him and he'd lose everything he had fought for. Surely he must realize that. What if these political leaders had promised him everything he wanted? And why would they? What were they using him for?

Later than night, Maya had trouble sleeping, reviewing all she had learned and read that day. She walked out onto the terrace. Joseph was there and she stopped, wondering whether to retreat quietly rather than disturb him. Then she remembered what his mother had said, that he was bothered by something and she should talk with him. So, she stayed, *"I couldn't sleep either, Joseph. Do you mind if I join you?"*

Joseph didn't turn around, just quietly said, *"It's getting worse. I hardly seem to be able to sleep at all anymore."*

"Why, Joseph? What is it that disturbs your sleep so much?"

"I'm changed, Maya. This Bahama's world has changed me."

She stood close, but not too close. He was so deep in thought, she wanted him to feel her presence, not see her. He needed to look out to the horizon, and she wanted him to continue opening up to her. *"How have you changed?"*

"I can't seem to feel the inner peace anymore. And the spirits have been quiet. They don't talk to me anymore."

"Have you angered them?"

"Yes, I fear I have. I thought I was doing right. But maybe I've made a mistake. As a Hopi, I consider that natural phenomenon characteristically follows the laws of cause and effect. I also believe that, on occasion, when there's sufficient reason and when circumstances are favorable, man can influence those phenomena. Through our thoughts, we can affect the life and bodily welfare of another person. If our thoughts and wishes toward that person are right and good, they will have beneficial effects on both of us. There are millions of people I wish well, but I need to reach them. And, I need to do it quickly. Am I wrong to do it the way I do? Can't rooms full of people, radio or TV interviews, and newspaper articles be as effective as one on one? I fear the spirits may be angry that I seem to be getting sidetracked in my work."

"What do you mean?"

"I am talking to some people, making plans to reach the people on an even larger scale, to really affect their lives in many ways."

"What kind of plans?" She needed to act as if she didn't already know the secret he seemed to want to keep from her. Maybe she could help. Or, given her assignment, she may have to hurt him.

"I'd rather not say just yet, in case it doesn't happen – in case the plans fall through."

"All right. You can tell me when you're ready."

"But I sense the spirits are angry. Even during the ritual dance at the kiva, no spirit came to me. There is always a spirit that takes over my body. But this last time, I was empty, what some would call an 'empty or hollow soul'. That can only mean one thing – that my life is almost over. If the spirits have abandoned me – then they feel I have abandoned them. And that, by prophecy, means my death."

"I don't understand."

"The prophecy is that if the Pahana abandons his belief or his religion, he must die."

"My God!" Maya was getting alarmed. Was Joseph acting depressed and suicidal? *"I thought the Hopi believed in immortality. Your people need you. The spirits wouldn't kill you, how could they?"*

"Yes, we believe in immortality through the spirit."

"Do you mean reincarnation?"

"No, immortality through the spirit. There is no dividing line between life now and life later. They are the same. The spirit is

strong, even though you can't see it. It even leaves the body temporarily, and then returns, like in dreams. But in a larger way, a spirit journey without the body may occur at a critical time, as in an illness, when you're on the edge of death."

Joseph turned to face her. *"Besides the spirits wouldn't kill me, someone else would. I feel I have only a little time left. I don't feel the strength and support of the spirits. And I don't know if they'll come back."* His face reflected his fear.

"Joseph, perhaps we left the reservation too soon. We should go back and give you a chance to pray there and try to reach the spirits."

"A break is a good idea. Maybe I'm just tired. Come with me, not to the reservation, but to my place in Washington. We'll take a couple of weeks to unwind and regroup. There are some people there I need to see.

"People that are more important than the spirits?"

"No, but I need to see them first. I need them to reassure me that the plans are what they seem. Then I'll ask the spirits if it's all right."

His face and body reflected his exhaustion.

"Why don't you try to rest now, Joseph? We can leave for Washington first thing in the morning."

CHAPTER 20

WASHINGTON, D.C.

Washington, D.C. was sunny, cool and comfortable. It was nearing the end of summer. Maya and Joseph were in a cab on route to his apartment.

"My apartment is small, but comfortable, not fancy, because that's me. I have two bedrooms, so you'll have any privacy you need. It's not much, but it's home."

Joseph's apartment was the same one he had occupied for over a decade, for as a legal representative of the American Indian world, he needed to be on site at the white man's nation's capital, but his budget was minimal. The building was old, just one representation among others in a most depreciating section of the city. In the summer months the apartment was suffocating, and during the winter it was exceedingly cold, results of inefficient, ancient heating elements, no insulation and rattling windows in need of caulking, permitting cold winds to whip inside as though invited.

Indeed, the rooms within these antiquated walls held sparce furniture purchased near the turn of the last century. There was a small galley-type kitchen, with older appliances. She was surprised to see signs of gourmet cooking – a lot of spices and several gourmet cookbooks. One of the many sides of Joseph she would discover, no doubt. The bathroom fixtures looked so old she was surprised to find anything worked. There was a make-shift circular rod and curtain for a shower, over an old ball'n'claw tub. It has been many years since she had seen such a simple, basic apartment, that reflected absolutely none of its occupant's personality. There was only one picture hanging on the walls – a picture of a kachina dancer, what else?

"What are these, Joseph?" In the living room, she had found a couple of items that were obviously Indian.

"These articles are for the Hopi who travels away from home. This small clay pot symbolizes the one given to the Hopi during migration. It will always provide food and water when buried in the ground. These crystals I keep inside the pot are to provide the light I need to see my way. And this eagle feather is to remind me to pray and to send my messages to the Creator by the eagle messenger. They may seem simple, but it is my way. And it reminds me of my real home and my people.

"Why don't we get unpacked and settled for the night? It's getting late."

Maya got as settled in the small spare bedroom as she could. She decided to carry her toiletries into the bathroom only as she needed them, so her presence here wouldn't seem so obvious. She stood in the small room, looking at her bottle of shampoo in her hand, wondering why she didn't want to be obvious. *'Was this her way of handling what could be an awkward situation – a man and a woman together in one small apartment? Was she perhaps trying not to seem obvious so he wouldn't feel crowded? Or was she the one who was feeling uncomfortable?'*

She looked at herself in the small mirror over the dresser. *'All right, so you feel sort of uncomfortable about this. So what? You're here – handle it.'*

Maya realized the apartment was too quiet – she didn't hear Joseph moving around. She peeked into his bedroom and saw he had fallen asleep, lying on top of his bed, still dressed in his suit. Quietly, she moved to cover him. She looked at his peaceful, sleeping face. He looked almost beautiful to her. This man was becoming very important to Maya. She wanted to touch his face, but didn't dare wake him. She covered him and left the room.

Maya was beginning to recognize her strong feelings for Joseph. That night, after a long, relaxing bath, she investigated her nude body. She never had a weight problem from pregnancy; she lost the full eighteen pounds she had gained immediately after her son's birth. The only reminder was a fuller bust and a slightly larger pelvis, with a noticeable bulge in her pubic area that wasn't there before. Her stomach was still flat, tight as a long-distance swimmer's. In all, her body still looked youthful, strong and admittedly, fairly sexy. She wondered if Joseph would agree.

The next morning, they made plans for the day. *"I need to set up some meetings, so I'll be busy on the phone most of today. I'd like to make a special dinner for us tonight,"* he blushed slightly. *"I hope you don't mind. I'm a pretty good cook – one of my nontraditional, non-Indian hobbies. I know, Indian men don't cook. Well, I do. Is it all right if I surprise you?"*

Maya smiled. He was like a child, asking permission to do something. She was positive that he would be looking, maybe even asking, for her critique after dinner. His sensitivity touched her.

"I have some errands to do. Why don't I plan to be back here around three o'clock? Is that okay?" She did have to stop and check in with Tanner. She wasn't looking forward to his snide remarks when he found out where she was staying, and with whom.

"Okay, it's a deal. Three o'clock it is. Dinner at six, all right? But you're not allowed in the kitchen while I work. Agreed?"

She found herself wanting to reach out and hug him, thinking that this sharing of an apartment may not be so uncomfortable after all.

Tanner proved to be the uncomfortable one. He could be

brusque sometimes, and it didn't help that he seemed to be in a bad mood. *"Living with the guy? Did I hear you right? What the hell are you doing, Maya? I asked you to sleep with him, not play house with him!"* Tanner's face was so red it seemed to swell as if he were a volcano about to erupt.

"Calm down, Tanner. I thought this was what you wanted. I can watch him all the time. What do you want from me?" She had to turn her back on him before she said something she'd regret. She made believe she was looking at something outside the window. But she had to add one more thing, without turning around. *"Besides I haven't slept with him. I'm staying in his spare bedroom."*

"Yeah, right. And I have red hair."

"Damn you, Tanner," she turned around to face him, feeling her face getting flushed with anger. *"Stop acting like an asshole, or I'll begin to believe you really are one! I don't go to bed with just anybody – or I would have with you long ago."* She stopped, thinking maybe she went a little too far with that one.

Tanner put his hands up to signal 'enough', *"All right, sorry. I overreacted, okay?"*

She sighed, collapsing in the nearest chair. *"I really don't know what to think, Elliott. Maybe I'm the wrong person for this job."*

"No, you're not. I'm sure of that. You've got to play spy, Maya. I want you to go through his apartment. You've got a job to do, girl! Please don't go soft on me. Don't fall in love with the guy." Tanner was behind his desk, standing, leaning over, looking down at her.

Maya hung her head, looking at her lap, *"It may be too late for that. I don't know if I can do this, Elliott."*

Tanner straightened up, taking a deep breath, *"Jesus,*

Maya. Don't tell me that! You're the only one I can count on. You have to do this – what if I'm right? What if he's using you, using all of us? He could know you're working with us. And he may be using you to throw up a smoke screen, to keep us guessing. He could be working you over, Maya!" He stopped when he saw she was getting angry again. Her face, as she stood up, showed it clearly. Good, he thought, he needed to make her want to prove him wrong.

"Damn you, Tanner." She walked out, slamming the door. Her usual exit, it seemed.

Maya needed to take a long walk to try and sort out some things in her head. Yes, she was on an assignment. And yes, she was getting emotionally involved. But it had been a long time since her feelings had been even recognizable. She had buried them so deep inside after losing her family, she'd forgotten what it was like to feel anything.

She sat in a small park near the apartment, watching young mothers with their infants and toddlers. She used to be like that – so loving, so patient, in wonder at every word and movement her son had made. He was such a marvel to her, so responsive and smart. She pictured him running down the sidewalk, arms upstretched yelling *"Daddy!"* into his father's big embrace. His father would kiss his face, giving him the giggles. She realized she was crying and had to stop before the deep sadness set in. Gathering herself together, she realized it was after four o'clock and wondered if Joseph would worry.

He called out to her as she let herself into the apartment. *"Don't come out here, I'm creating."* The air smelled wonderful, full of strong, spicey aromas. Within the hour, dinner was ready, and it was one of the best she'd had in a long time.

"You could open a gourmet restaurant with this kind of talent," she raved all through the meal. By the time they settled in front of the fire with some wine, he had a peaceful, happy look on

his face. She didn't want to ruin the mood, so they talked about happy things.

"The Hopi believes so strongly in the animal spirit, speaking with the Indian in unspoken messages and understanding the same. If you were to be an animal, Joseph, which one would it be?"

Joseph looked pensively into the fire for a moment, then turned to her with a grin, *"I would be a fox – taking care of my family and hunting for our food. I would be sly and smart in the way I dealt with other animals and beings."* He laughed, *"That is not an easy question to answer. There are so many animals."*

"What animal do you think I would be? And why?" she asked him.

He looked closely into her face. The fire seemed to make his dark eyes sparkle and dance. He reached over and stroked her cheek, *"A rabbit. Smart and quick, soft and cuddly. And delicious to eat."*

He leaned closer and kissed her, lightly at first, then harder and more demanding. Before either of them realized it, they were tearing at each other's clothes. They made love on the rug in front of the fireplace. It was so intense and dramatic, that after they were done, neither of them was able to move for a while.

They lay side by side, and he reached for her hand, *"I've been wanting you for so long, Maya."* His voice was no more than a whisper. *"You are in my dreams, in all my waking thoughts. I never wanted a woman before, it's all so new to me. But it seems so natural, so right."*

He lifted himself on one elbow to look at her face and realized she was crying, softly and quietly. *"What are you afraid of? Or did I hurt you?"*

"No, you didn't hurt me." She looked lovingly up into his

face. *"I've wanted you too. But I'm so scared of loving and losing all over again. The time I lost my husband and son, I didn't know if I would ever recover. That kind of caring again scares me, Joseph."*

"I'm afraid too. I'm afraid of not having you in my life. I'm afraid of disappointing you or making you angry. I'm afraid of not pleasing you."

He leaned over and began kissing her again. This time, they made love slowly, anticipating one another, experimenting with touches, trying to make it last forever.

That night, he slept peacefully, hardly moving. She lay beside him, in his bedroom with the larger bed, watching him. She felt happy and satisfied. She touched his scars. How deep they were. To anyone else, they would seem ugly. To her everything about him seemed perfect.

CHAPTER 21

WASHINGTON, D.C.

When she awoke, he was still lying beside her, quietly watching her. *"You look like a sweet, innocent, young girl when you're sleeping. Like a sleeping beauty."* He kissed her very lightly. *"Come and watch me cook a queen's breakfast for you."* But neither of them moved right away, as if there was something unsaid but understood between them. As he gazed into her eyes, he tenderly touched a curl that had fallen over her forehead. *"It's clear to me now that I have been moving towards you and you towards me for a long time. Though neither of us was aware of the other before, there was a kind of mindless certainty humming blithely along beneath our ignorance that ensured we would come together. Like two solitary eagles, flying the great prairies by celestial reckoning; all of these years and lifetimes, we have been moving towards one another."* She felt the same and wanted to hold this moment longer. But he moved, feeling shy once again after opening his heart.

As she watched him move like a dancer around the kitchen, they began to talk. Small talk gave way quickly to a subject she had been wanting to talk about. *"In your speeches, you talked about all of us learning to concern ourselves with right VS wrong. Sort of a question of ethics. Do you mind if we talk about it, even though it isn't exactly light breakfast talk?"*

His face looked so handsome and lively when he laughed, *"Okay. You know we haven't really had a serious discussion since we talked on the reservation. Go ahead."*

Maya's face grew serious, *"I grew up in the late 60's,*

through the early 80's, where there was a lot of talk about ethics. After the assassinations of John Kennedy, Martin Luther King Jr., and Bobby Kennedy, another movement seemed to replace ethics, especially because of the Vietnam War. We became cynical, and our concern turned to watching out for ourselves. Now we seem to evaluate ourselves by whether we've reached our aspirations, rather than on how good we are. I guess you could call it all a Yuppie version of success – like who are you, how much do you make, etc. How do we change our philosophy from 'Greed is good'?"

Joseph answered, *"And how do we change from the philosophy of 'as long as it's legal, it's ethical,' right? We tend to think, in American society today, that everything is defined in the Internal Revenue Codebook. People seem to be proud when they find loopholes and evade taxes in their own 'legitimate' way. Then it is somehow rationalized or their behavior is justified by it being just 'an exception'. So many people in business and government seem to live for achieving those 'exceptions'. We can find an excuse for everything it seems. It brings to mind the notion used so often, 'honesty is the best policy' or 'good ethics is good business'. What they don't realize is they are talking business, not ethics."*

"So, where do we look for answers – religion?"

"Ethics can still be defined as behavior that helps people and society. There still exist actions like compassion, honesty, fairness, accountability. Those can still be recognized as universal, ethical values. The essence of ethics is our level of caring. That's what sets us aside as human beings. The essence of the Golden Rule has been around a long time. Greek and Chinese culture recognized it thousands of years before Christ articulated his version. But ethics has two dimensions – one is practical, one spiritual. People have an inherent, inner sense of right and wrong. There is a theory that says 'you do what you can to make differences in the network of people that you affect.' You

bring some happiness, some joy, remove some pain. We all have that responsibility. We all affect people – but we don't do as good a job as we should."

"Why?"

"We as individuals forget. Some more than others. We need to think about our own personal approaches to ethics. We read about it. And then we make decisions on how to act as a person. We should look at all facets of our lives in a problem-solving manner. Offer up three alternative actions – and search out that one which is ethical. It will be there – and easy to recognize. That's the practice we use in the seminar you saw. And I think it helps people."

"But isn't that attitude easier said than done? What if you're home one night and a young woman knocks on your door. And you open it and she asks you to hide her, because a mean-looking man was following her. Then when he knocks on your door and asks if she's there – what do you do?"

"It's all right to say you haven't seen her. Then close the door and lock it."

"What if he demands your money? Can I say I have none? What is my rationalization process?"

"Rationalization process," he laughed. "You mean is it okay to lie?" She nodded. "Lying against injury is an ethical rule. On a daily basis, we are faced with decisions of self-interest VS doing the right thing. That's the reality of life. What we all need to ask ourselves is, 'do we have the strength to do the right thing'? Or, 'do we start rationalizing?'"

"Help me out here. Give me a simple description of ethics."

"Okay, let me put it in simple terms. The only way you will get what you want is to have a good set of values as to what's important and mix that with doing the right thing. You don't need to overdramatize this – just look at the cost of your actions. It can really be that simple"

"Your highest aspiration seems to be to have the best society that we can. From caring and generosity, fairness and accountability will come. Which all means, we will be making decisions differently than we have in a long time. Do you really think it can happen, that we can all change that much?"

"We have no choice. This country is 'going down the tubes'. To survive, we must change. And we must do it soon."

"But how are you going to do it?"

"I don't know that I can. I'm trying to get people to think – but I don't know if they will. Maybe I'll fail. If I do, then that means I'll be dead. And someone else will need to do it – or we'll all die."

They were both remembering their conversation on the terrace, where he said he was going to be killed. The air between them became suddenly quiet and awkward.

"Joseph, do you still think you will die soon?"

"Maybe. I don't know. All I know is that I was given a mission. And you were sent to me. I knew you were coming. My spirit guides told me. But I don't think your mission is what you now think it is. You are more important in this than you realize. And, no, I haven't heard from the spirits lately."

"What can I do to help?"

"Believe in me. Many times, I feel I am struggling on my own. I perceive you don't believe in my spiritual guides, but please respect my belief in them. My deep commitment and belief in my purpose must, essentially, set me apart from all other humans. But what matters also to me is your support. You don't have to agree, or even understand. Just please believe in me. Or, I will not survive."

"Yes, you will. You don't need me – you started all of this when you were born. And you will carry on after I leave."

"I have accomplished a great deal. I have spread the word, so to speak. But I do need you, more than you know. Now, I think we should talk about the weather."

They sat quietly for a moment, looking at each other over their coffee. It wasn't exactly uncomfortable. As a matter of fact, she found that looking across a breakfast table at this man was becoming too comfortable. She moved out of her chair and turned her back on him as she began washing the dishes. *'What was she doing? Was she really ready to love this man? What about finding out his true motives, and her need to prove Tanner wrong? How much of this had to do with Tanner and the job she had to do?'* God, how she needed to get alone for a while so she could think.

"Joseph, would you mind if I went back home to Boston for a few days? There are some things there I need to take care of." She didn't dare look at him in case he might read doubt on her face.

Joseph came up behind her, smoothing her hair, but only lightly touching it as if it were holy and he might spoil it. *"Are you running away, Maya? Have I scared you away?"*

She leaned back against his warm, now-familiar body, as she had yearned to that night on the mesa. *"No, I'm not running away. I'll only be gone a couple of days."* She turned around so she could look into his eyes. *"So much has been happening with us, I need to be able to breathe for a while. And to think. I want to make sure that what is happening between us is good for us. And whether I can really handle it. I'm sorry, Joseph. I need to get away to deal with this."*

"Don't leave me now, Maya. I feel as though I can't exist if you're not here beside me. Such a strange sensation – I'm not sure if you're inside of me or I'm inside of you. I think we're both

inside of another being we have created called 'us'. We ARE that being. We have both lost ourselves and created something else, something that exists only as an interlacing of the two of us. Neither of us exists independent of that being."

"I'll only be gone a couple of days, Joseph."

"And when you return, what will you say to me?" She could read on his face that he was both confused and scared. This must be such a new sensation to him, never having loved like this before.

"I'll either tell you that I love you – or – that I can't love you."

"You're scaring me, Maya. You're running away from me. What can I do to change your mind?"

"I haven't given you my choice yet. Please, try to understand. There is much more involved here than you know about."

"All right. But it'll be a very long few days, because I do love you."

He kissed her to keep her from saying any more.

CHAPTER 22

BOSTON

Maya was feeling very irritated. There was a loud, rather obnoxious child seated nearby on the plane who was complaining and whining with every breath. Damn, how that was irritating. And, behind her there were a couple of men from, she guessed, the Middle East somewhere. And they were jabbering as if they had never talked before and were making up for the lost years. What was wrong with her to make her so irritable? Even waiting at the airport had given her problems. She wouldn't let Joseph go with her. Such a long, extended farewell would have been too sad. She had a thirty-minute wait before boarding and had felt her heart racing, which made her feel faint and weak. Either she was just exhausted or starting menopause fifteen years too early.

She needed to think. And she craved alone time. She still had an hour to sit on this plane, becoming more irritated. Maybe she could isolate herself a little. She asked the steward for a set of earphones, and found some classical music, closing her eyes. It didn't take long for her nerves to settle.

There was so much jumbled inside her head. She needed to sort out her thoughts. She wondered if she should really be helping the F.B.I. Maya had been properly trained, proving to be physically and mentally strong. And she had helped them in several rather sticky situations. There had been several Native American riots where she had advised them how to handle the Indians. They had always listened to her – at first. The government VS Native American Culture – there would be some sort of negotiation to end the situation. Then they would reach a compromise. Maya was never happy with the outcome. Either the

Indians would have to give in too much, in her opinion, or the government would renege on the agreement. Not always. But even once would have been too much for her.

But, unlike Tanner, she hadn't been hardened by it all. Maybe that was because, in between assignments, she had her work at the Museum. And for a while, she had her family. The memories made her smile.

On one of the rare occasions her father was home in Boston, he went to a young eye doctor recommended by one of his coworkers at the Museum. That night, he brought the doctor home for dinner. Her father had seen something in this young man and wanted him to meet Maya. She was almost twenty-six then, and she figured her father was worried she was becoming an old maid.

Maya had been satisfied and comfortable with her life, working in the Anthropology Department at the Museum, part-time teaching at the university, and doing occasional jobs for the F.B.I. By some people's standards, she had a full life.

But she was too serious, her father had said. She needed to laugh more, and not be so particular about men. What men? She felt the ones she had met were either too stupid and infantile-acting, or very boring. The only one who either made her laugh or made her mad was Tanner.

And so, they sat at the dinner table, her father, mother, Maya and this young doctor. And she laughed so much, she could hardly eat. Her father had such insight into people. Such an amazing man. He just knew. This man was just right for her. He made her laugh. Her father was right, as always.

This young doctor was charmed too. He kept seeing her. And she found herself smiling all the time. And so, when he made love to her the first time, he'd asked her to marry her. And it seemed right. And it was.

Unfortunately, there had been signs that all would not always be right and happy. They had made wedding plans but had to keep changing them. With so many relatives, mostly on his side, someone wouldn't be able to come on that particular date, then someone else on the next date they'd set. And then, her mother died.

Her mother. A warm, quiet woman that hardly ever talked. It was hard for Maya to remember much about her mother. Except that she was a dark beauty, very French. Never seemed to offer much in the way of advice, just was more of a listener. Her mother would accept things as they were, as if there had been no choice. So, she would just smile, and say '*all right*'. And it would be accepted.

In all of those years of marriage, Maya's parents were only together about two to three months out of each year. No wonder Maya was an only child. And her mother would quietly accept it all. Not a very '*modern woman*', in Maya's eyes.

There was a balance to Maya, bits and pieces of each parent. She had some of her mother's passiveness and acceptance, and some of her father's more aggressive strengths. But, too many times, her mother's influence of quiet, seriousness would prevail. And her father would try to change that. He succeeded with her young man.

After her mother died, Maya and Doctor Tony decided to just elope. She no longer wanted a big wedding – one of her mother's wants, not really hers. Then, they wrote to all of the relatives, mostly his, that they wanted it that way and hoped everyone would understand. They didn't. And they took every opportunity to remind the young couple how they had made such a mistake. And especially in Italian families, the young bride is always proud to take her husband's name. Another unforgiving event.

When the baby came along, all was forgiven. Maya took a

deep sigh as she relaxed in her airplane seat, isolated from those around her. With her eyes still closed, she could see herself giving birth, as if it were a news reel. And Tony, so pale and worried, trying to remember his Lamaze training. Some Doctor!

The baby, after two full days of hard labor, was perfect. So sweet, so small and delicate, and so much hair! The nurses all loved him – he was so cute. And how he loved to surprise them. He flipped over in his little clear bassinet in the hospital nursery, one arm dangling and caught over the side, with a puzzled look on his face. The nurses may even still be talking about him, five years later.

Maya had been in heaven, two wonderful guys in her life. Tony was a loving, wonderful husband and father. He doted on his son, Frank. The name was a compromise, named after both grandfathers, Franko Adonna and Francois Chardon. But he looked like Grandpa Chardon. At least to Maya.

She had concentrated on her baby. No museum work. No F.B.I. Nothing but her baby. Tony loved little Frankie, but kept telling Maya she '*coddled*' him too much. How can you give too much love to a child? Too many hugs and kisses? No way.

She could feel the tears start, but she had to remember it all. They had started fighting. Tony wanted another baby. She felt it was too soon, and Frankie wasn't ready. At three years old, he needed her too much to share her with anyone else. '*Was she wrong? Was it all her fault?*' It was almost too painful to remember.

They had been yelling – well, Tony was yelling and she was trying to respond. Then Frankie had started crying, running to his mother, hugging her leg. Tony realized the yelling was too loud and tried to comfort Frankie. But Frankie kept pushing him away, kept hugging his Mother's leg. They all finally calmed down, and Frankie let his Daddy hold him. He wanted ice cream. Ice cream was always what he needed, when Mommy and Daddy upset him.

But there was none in the house. She needed to be alone, so Daddy took Frankie to get ice cream. And never came home. A drunk driver killed them just minutes later. And suddenly she had become totally alone.

Maya reached into her bag for Kleenex. She had heard that everyone needed to cry. That salty tears were filled with toxins from your body, and that it was good for you to release them. Then why didn't she feel better when she cried?

She needed to feel better. And Joseph made her feel better than she had felt in over two years. Damn the F.B.I.! *'Why wasn't she facing the fact that she loved this man and needed him? Why be afraid of caring again? Of feeling good again?'* Yes, maybe she'll get hurt. But she could enjoy it while it lasted. And he needed and loved her.

She opened her eyes. She had been so stupid and blind. You can't live on memories. You can't reach out and hug memories. That was her mother. Make your new memories – that was her father. *'Okay, Dad, I will,'* she said inside her mind. She would quit the F.B.I. and devote herself to Joseph.

But, as she looked out her plane's window, she realized she was headed the wrong way. She was almost to Boston, and he was back in Washington.

She'd go home for tonight, check the mail in the morning, and return to Washington by late afternoon. And she'd surprise Joseph by returning a day early and tell him she loved him. And they'd live happily ever after. As long as it lasted, anyway.

The cab ride back in Washington the next day wasn't moving fast enough for her. Maya couldn't wait to see Joseph. As she ran up the outside steps, she didn't see the men watching her from their parked car. As she fumbled with her keys inside the hallway, she heard voices from inside, which meant Joseph was there – and that's all she cared about.

In the next few seconds, everything changed. It changed so abruptly that she felt faint, and she could hear her heart racing in her ears.

Joseph's living room was full of men – strangers. But some had familiar faces – those same political faces. And, then they all left. Within sixty seconds, without words, the room was empty except for Joseph and Maya. She had walked in on a political meeting, obviously. In seconds, she was brought back to reality. He must tell her his plans now.

"What's going on, Joseph? Who were those men?"

Joseph wouldn't look at her, *"Just some friends and business associates."*

Then he came towards her, *"I'm so glad you're back. And early. I missed you."*

As he held her in his arms, she didn't know whether to laugh or cry. *'Why couldn't he just tell her? What would he say if she told him she already knew his plans?'* Except for his motives. *'What should she do? Why couldn't he trust her? He said he loved her. Did he lie? Was he just using her?'*

She had to act normally, no matter what. *'Was all that heart-wrenching decision-making on the plane just a waste of time?'* *"I couldn't make a decision yet, Joseph. I just missed you."* And that much was true.

Normal…she had to act normal and get through this. But she felt so numb. Her fingers, her legs – all felt cold and numb on the outside, while inside she was falling apart.

CHAPTER 23

ON STAKEOUT

F.B.I. Agent Peter Weatherford had his nose buried in the newspaper, as usual. He had this habit of making little sounds when he was reading, which really irritated his partner, Agent Niehardt. This time, his little noises sounded like a puppy whimpering. *"Jesus, man. Will you stop reading that paper? You're driving me nutso!"*

"But Ralph, things are really getting pretty scary, all these disasters…" He stopped suddenly when Niehardt put his hand up in Weatherford's face, palm towards his nose.

"Look, there she is again, going into this Pahana's building." They both watched the beautiful young woman until she was inside, out of sight. Niehardt wet his lips, *"I never knew we had any agents that looked like that."*

"Are you sure that's her?"

"Look, Weatherford, she's the only one hanging around the guy. And Tanner said she was the only woman even near Pahana. That has to be her. Man, what duty – inside, 'under-cover' surveillance." Then, he enjoyed a good laugh at Maya's expense. *"I'll tell you, after this job is done, I'm lookin' her up. She is exceptional."*

"Right, Niehardt, another notch for your belt. Jesus, what are you doing anyway, trying out for 'stud of the month?'"

Niehardt joined in the joke, *"No, 'stud of the year'."*

No sooner had they finished laughing, and Weatherford had his face surrounded by the newspaper and he began whimpering again. Suddenly, he stopped and cleared his throat, *"Jeez, listen to this…"*

"Do I have to?"

"Look, I listen to you and your stud stories without complaining. You listen to me for a change. This article may just wake you up." He began reading aloud before Niehardt could protest again, *"'Several volcanoes have formed and been active over the past year, forming what look like islands southwest of Mexico. These pieces of new land look like stepping stones from the Continent almost to the islands of Hawaii. Geologists say the significance of this event may be the latest in the Pacific Ocean's tempestuous Ring of Fire. Virtually all the land areas that border the Pacific Ocean – from the west coast of South America north to Alaska, through the Aleutians over to Japan, and south to Indonesia and New Zealand – have been the victims of relentless geological violence since the dawn of history. Along this vast arc, more than three-quarters of the world's major earthquakes occur. And here too, more than half of the planet's 600 active volcanoes are located. The forces behind the Ring of Fire remained unknown until the theory of plate tectonics, or continental drift, came to prominence in the 1960s. Studies since then have confirmed that the earth's crust is split into a number of thick rock plates. The plates beneath the Pacific Ocean are in slow but continuous motion, in some places forcing their way under adjacent continental plates'."* Here, he took a deep breath, feeling weak, a knot forming in his stomach.

"They go on and tell about the cause of volcanic activity. And there's the result of this – listen, 'As often happens when an earthquake originates under the ocean floor, the greatest damage to life and property is caused not by the quake itself but by the tsunami, or giant sea wave, that the quake sets in motion. The floods that follow are so immense that it seems as though God

was threatening a second deluge, or all things were returning to original chaos. The latest disasters resulting from this volcanic island formation and quaking recalls the calamities of the Roman Empire. In that age, when extraordinary events were routinely attributed to God's will and disasters were viewed as divine punishment for man's sins, such volcanic and quake activity caused astonishment and fear throughout the decaying Roman Empire. Because of the extensive flooding in the Hawaiian Islands and along the southwestern Continental shores and the resulting spread of new and terrifying disease, we must pause and reflect for a moment – have we committed some monstrous sin? And will it end soon? Those who study such catastrophe say they don't know if it will end at all."

The knot in Weatherford's stomach was tightening, *"Then, there are these other stories on the continuous flooding and further spread of the new strain of virus, still killing people. What is happening? And why, Ralph?"*

"You are so fuckin' naïve, man. All that is called sensationalism. To sell more newspapers, they really build up these news items, makin' it seem so much worse than it really is. Jesus, man, you better stop readin' that stuff. It'll give you ulcers."

"I think it already has," Weatherford was wishing the spreading pain in his stomach would go away. There was something wrong about all of this, and he just couldn't stop worrying about it.

CHAPTER 24

WASHINGTON, D.C.

Maya was reading the same newspaper article. Only her interest went beyond just the words – there was far more meaning in the emergence of these new islands southwest of Mexico. She knew she had to talk to Joseph about it tonight. She felt sure it was part of the prophecy. She needed to know what it all meant.

But first, she had to search the apartment before she went to Tanner's office. She didn't find anything unusual, until she spied a shoebox hidden in his closet. She sat on his bed with the spilled contents, trying to make sense of what was important and what wasn't. There were a series of ticket stubs for an airline, all roundtrip from various places around the U.S. to Chicago. It appeared he had gone to Chicago eight times from January to June at two-week intervals. In other words, something was significant about Chicago. She lay them out and took pictures with her camera, then returned everything to the closet.

Joseph had a great many books on politics. She took note of what they were. Some were histories of how past Presidents of the U.S. had campaigned, the how's of political *'lying'* and several on international political concerns and anthologies. This was pretty heavy reading for someone *'not very interested'* in politics.

When she had completed the search of his apartment, she just sat on her bed, thinking. She didn't know what was happening, and she didn't even know how she felt about it. Maya just knew she loved Joseph, she felt miserable, and she was very scared about all of this. She needed Tanner now – he could explain all of this to her. She hoped.

Tanner looked up in surprise when she walked into his office. She didn't say anything at first, just put the film on his desk and sat in a chair, leaning on one hand which supported her forehead.

"What is this?"

"This is what you wanted – all that I could find in Joseph's apartment."

"What are the pictures of?"

She sat up, trying not to appear emotional about it all – she was only spying on the man she loved. *"Before Joseph left this morning, I went through his wallet. There was a weird-looking white I.D. card that I took pictures of, both sides. Something to do with the Defense Department. Really strange. And a piece of paper I found, with the words OP-COUP, and a phone number. Then some airline ticket stubs for trips to Chicago, every two weeks. I really don't know what any of this means – but I do know he's serious about running for President. And I think all of this fits in somehow."* She felt so exhausted, feeling the stress and strain of this job more than any she ever had before.

Tanner held the film in his hands, knowing he should have it developed in their lab there immediately. But, he also could see his friend was in deep pain, *"Maya, what is it?"*

Her body slowly slouched way down into the chair, *"It's as if I've cracked a door, searching, peeking, and the light is streaming from that door. And I'm yearning to get to it, to push it back, to go beyond it, full into the reality that lies in that light. But a part of me wants to push it closed, make it dark again, away from what I would find there."* She looked up at Tanner. *"This whole case scares me. I feel like I don't really know what's going on."* She saw his face, and immediately sat up, *"Tanner, you know something you haven't told me."*

"I can't, Maya. It's better for you not to know. Trust me." He

started for the door, holding up the undeveloped film so she'd know what was taking him away from their conversation. *"Be right back."*

So, this was to be another tense encounter when he would tell her only a portion of what he knew. While she sat waiting, thinking, she became angry. She was tired of being kept in the dark and fed only bits and crumbs Tanner chose to throw her way. Somehow in the midst of all this crumb scattering and gathering, she was supposed to get enough and be satisfied. Not this time. The stakes were too high. It was her life they were talking about now, because somehow she was going to see Joseph through this. She waited a lifetime for him, and he for her. No one was going to ruin it now. Not again, especially not this time. She had lost it all before and this time she would lose herself, too. She couldn't let that happen.

By the time Tanner returned several minutes later, her mind was set. She sat up straight in her chair, silently staring at him.

Tanner could feel her tension. He knew he'd probably give in to her. But he had to fight it as long as he could. He shouldn't risk more danger for her. *"It's highly classified – above Top Secret."*

"I'm not leaving until you tell me."

"Jesus, Maya. Don't do this."

"Tell me about the white card." She waited. He didn't move or speak. *"You know you have to, Elliott,"* she spoke quietly, leaning over his desk, reaching to touch his hand. *"Tell me,"* she whispered.

He took a deep breath. All right. She already knew too much. Besides, she had a right to know. He reached into a deep desk drawer and pulled out the file. He took a non-assigned white care out of the file and gave it to her.

She noticed the card was white with red borders on both sides. On one side were spaces for height, weight, a card number, and the seal of the U.S. Department of Defense. On the other side were the words, Federal Emergency Assignee, Office of Emergency Planning, a space for the cardholder's name and signature, and this sentence, '*The person described on this card has been assigned essential emergency duties for the federal government. It is imperative that the bearer be assisted in travel by the fastest means to this emergency assignment.*'

"They're used for special projects. For instance, when the U.S. Office of Censorship was first started, they actually had the same exact cards and met at the same place, on the campus of Western Maryland College. By the time the group was called Maritime Information Security Program (MISP), they had real offices. But they used the same cards and everything."

Tanner sat back in his chair, rubbing his eyes, *"Maybe it's tied in with the President and has his sanction."* He really knew better than that. *"Until we know more, here's what you need to do. Hang on for a second…"* He left the room again, returning with a small package.

He handed the package to her, which was marked '*Surveillance Disc*'. *"You stick this portable mini-microphone on the inside of Joseph's lapel and I'll have a unit out there at the campus tomorrow taping the meeting. That'll tell us more about what he's up to. And I'll check into some things at my end, while you just stay cool about this, okay?"*

Maya opened the small surveillance package, *"You mean I just stick this little disc on him? And then I patiently sit on my hands and wait for you to call?"*

"That's it."

"I'll put this disc on him. But, right now, Elliott, the rest of the story." She was interrupted by a knock on the office door. The

pictures. Tanner spread them on his desk. She reached over, picking one up. *"You can start with this."* She held it up.

Tanner sat back, knowing he had to tell her all. *"All right. The Top Secret file is called Operation Coup, or OP-COUP, as on this piece of paper,"* taking the picture she had held up. *"And the phone number is the private line for the C.I.A. Director, Arthur Pinkerton. Your Joseph Pahana is in the middle of a planned overthrow of the President. Those trips to Chicago,"* as he motioned to her pictures of the ticket stubs, *"were strategy sessions. David Gordon has a house there, outside of town. It's a wooded retreat, perfect for isolation and privacy, and easily protected by the guards. Guards, which by the way, are definitely C.I.A. As a matter of fact, we also have two men assigned to guard Joseph. You don't see them – but they're there. Just like these C.I.A. guards, they play the role of Secret Service-type agents – blend in but protect."*

He saw the set of her jaw, saw the hint of tears in her eyes, but continued. She needed to hear it all.

"Apparently the Attorney General has suspected something like this for awhile. She doesn't trust Gordon or the DCI. The report's in a green file with a red tab, called OP-COUP, but also marked XGDS, meaning 'above top secret', with limited distribution, exempted from General Declassification Schedule. In other words, never gets put on the 'conveyor belt' for automatic declassification. If anything happens, the file gets shredded – automatically. This is because the people involved are mostly government people. The old government adage of cover and protect yourself. Unless they want to prosecute. Which they won't do. How do you prosecute your own government officials without looking like an ass?

"You see," Tanner sat back down behind his desk, *"the DCI is appointed by the President, to coordinate all the government-wide intelligence machinery. How would it look if the man that the President appointed is shown to be plotting against*

him? Not too good.

"So there you are. The President doesn't know yet. That's because we're playing a waiting game to find out who's really running this show. It couldn't be either Gordon or Pinkerton. When we get enough proof, they'll likely tell, not ask the DCI to step down to be replaced. The rest of them will simply be reabsorbed back into their jobs. And those with the opposition will simply look for another candidate."

"Is David Gordon still advising the President?"

"For the moment, yes." He leaned forward, with a glint in his eyes, "Just think of this coup, Maya. They're backing a man for President, who is supposedly very pious, deeply religious, a man representative of a minority ethnic group, but a man deeply committed and loyal to all Americans. Here is a man who has built a reputation for wanting to save peoples' souls and save the world. He is handsome and extremely intelligent. How can they lose? They put the right words in his mouth and guide him in the right direction. And I'll tell you, Maya, from everything I know of David Gordon – he really knows his stuff!

"The rest of the plans according to the file is they would go public with his candidacy around the first of the year. It reminds me of the 'Selling of the Presidency, 1968', how Nixon employed television and Madison Avenue techniques in his bid for President in 1968. But once in the White House, a President makes use of the same techniques to preserve and extend his power. There are only two men in this group who are proponents of that type of political strategy. The one who will get hurt most by all of this is Joseph Pahana. I hope he doesn't want to change things. Because it just doesn't work that way – no matter what they tell him."

"What do I do? Can't I try to warn him? How can I just sit there and not do anything?"

"Please, Maya, for now don't do anything. We'll be following Joseph and taping him. Put the disc on him and wait for my call. We'll take this a day at a time."

"Jesus, Tanner, when will you call me? I want to know what's happening just as badly as you do, Elliott!?

"I'll call when they bring me the tape tomorrow afternoon. I'll listen to some of it. If I think you need to hear it, I'll call you and we'll listen together. Fair enough?"

Maya's body slumped once more in her chair, "I guess that'll have to do."

Elliott Tanner reached over to put his hand over hers, "You've done a good job, Maya. I knew you'd come through."

"This one isn't easy, Elliott."

This time she left his office quietly. She would have felt better if she'd had something to yell at him for. Instead, she felt sick to her stomach. And very scared.

CHAPTER 25

THE APARTMENT

Maya got to the apartment before Joseph returned. She had stopped to purchase some groceries, hoping that the cooking would keep her busy and help distract her from thinking about things too much.

She heard Joseph at the door. "*Joseph, I've been waiting for you. Have you heard the news or read the paper?*"

"*No, I really haven't. I guess I've been so wrapped up in other things,*" then he saw her face, "*What is it? Your face is so pale. What's wrong?*" He sat down by her and took her hands.

"*Hon'hoya told me the stories of the four worlds of the Hopi. One of the things he said was the people of the Fourth World were told that after their Emergence, that if they 'preserved the memory and meaning of their Emergence, the stepping stones would emerge again to prove the truth of their journey.' Those footprints, the islands to the west and south, are reforming.*" She read him the same story from the paper that Weatherford had read that morning, "*Are these the island stepping stones that were foretold?*"

"*Yes.*"

"*What does it mean, Joseph?*"

"*It means that I'm running of time. And it's also a warning to me.*" Joseph sat forward and dropped his head into his hands, elbows on his knees, saying, "*No. No!*"

Maya was feeling both the effects of the last two days and

the fear of the disasters, and could see Joseph's action reflecting her own fears. She moved closer to him, dropping to her knees on the floor, cradling his head in her arms, trying to soothe him.

"Maybe we're overreacting, Joseph. Maybe it was just time for something like this to happen."

"No, it's a sign. The spirits are giving us a sign, Maya." He looked up at her with a stricken face. *"The spirits had granted me this prophecy. Such power. Power that comes as a gift always comes with strings, no, with chains, attached. I feel so weighted down by these chains, I feel that everything that happens now is my fault. All of this is either a warning of our world's destruction, or it has begun and won't stop until our world, as we now know it, is ended. Then the Fifth World will emerge."*

"I can't believe that, Joseph. There are too many people. The spirits wouldn't be that cruel. If that is really what is happening. It may not have anything to do with your spirits, Joseph."

He sat back, staring at her. *"You don't believe, do you? Even the island stepping stones prophecized, should show you proof. But still you don't believe in the prophecy."* His dark eyes stared at her. *"How could you act as if you believed, and all the time you didn't?"*

"I don't know what to believe anymore, Joseph. Too much has happened. I'm very confused. I know I'm disappointing you. I'm sorry. Please forgive me. The only real thing I can believe in is how I feel about you. No matter what happens, I love you. And I always will. And I know you believe in all of it with a passion. Passion is not something you can control all the time. I hope your passion will be contagious. I wish I could believe you were doing the right thing."

"You love me, but you can't believe in me and what I am doing?" Joseph stood up, looking down at her. *"I don't know what*

more I can say or do. You either believe in me or you don't."

"Maybe I've listened to white man's logic for so many years, it blocks my mind to simple belief. I want to understand, I really do. And I want to trust you. But too much has happened. And you don't trust me enough to share all of it with me. Trust and belief are a two-way street, Joseph." She stood up to face him. "Do you trust me enough to tell me about those men and what you're talking to them about?"

"I can tell you this much, Maya, that through these men I can rectify what has been done." His body seemed to swell with pride, "A rotten, terrible thing has been done to a small, naïve tribe of innocent original inhabitants of the Americas, and the magnanimous wealthy nation must make restitution."

"But the Hopi are still alive, your traditions and religion still in place, your land still intact. At least a part of it."

"For how long? So far, we have only discovered coal on our land. If we find anything – anything that is more valuable, we will lose it all. You know that. That's why I have been fighting cases of Indian property rights for ten years. If this country has to give back the land – even if we win half back, then that will provide protection for us. That is why this Hopi lawyer has been working with the Sioux in Dakota. I will never give up that fight, not until we win."

"You had a higher purpose in life. You said there is a difference between a hero and a celebrity. In your Hopi prophecy, you are a hero to your people. But you – you want to be a celebrity."

"No, Maya. I just have a job to do. We were all sacrificed by government big shots, who either had their hands in the cookie jar or were furthering their own political ambitions, or who were just plain liars abusing the trust that had been placed in them. It doesn't matter whether it was a century ago, a decade ago, three *months ago, or yesterday. It has to stop."*

"Joseph, the men you are meeting with are corrupt. Not everyone in Washington is corrupt – the vast majority are overworked, underpaid, dedicated bureaucrats – men and women, in the best sense, who try their best to sort out the problems of their myriad departments brought on by politicians waffling for votes. It isn't easy to just do your job here."

But Joseph wasn't listening, there was anger in his eyes, as his mouth began to curve into a crazed smile, to her it was the smile of a stranger, not her lover. "I am glad that I had the opportunity to live in the white man's world. All the better to use this knowledge to fight him for our rights. Knowing this government's strengths and weaknesses, I have an advantage."

They stood, staring at each other for what seemed like an eternity, before his face began to soften towards her, and he looked more like himself again. "I can't tell you any more because it may put you in danger. Can't you believe in me enough to accept that?"

"There's a being inside of you that I'm not good enough to bring out, not strong enough to reach. I sometimes have the feeling you've been here a long time, more than a lifetime. And you've dwelt in private places none of the rest of us have ever dreamed about. You frighten me, even though you're gentle. But you reach me – deep inside – where no one else has. If I didn't fight to control myself, I feel that I might lose my own center and never get back. But now, this moment, I need to be strong," she stood firmly, putting her hands on her hips for emphasis. "Tell me all that you are doing, or I may not be here tomorrow when you return."

His face looked like it would collapse, "Why? We are destined to be together. Why are you doing this?"

"Because I already know, Joseph. It would have helped if

you'd told me. If you'd shared with me. I know where you've been and I know who they are. I just wanted to hear it from your lips." She turned as if to walk away. Then, she seemed to think of something else. *"I am not who you think I am. I didn't come to Arizona only as an Anthropologist."*

"What do you mean?"

She could sense how stubborn they both were being – to assert an understanding of something before the thought was finished or to argue with a swift, irresistible impulse – stubbornness and pride, the things which often make dialogue impossible.

She bit her lip, she must not tell him everything. *"All I can say is I know. And, Joseph, I think you are wrong. Your spirits have abandoned you because you're wrong. You had a job to do and now you have forgotten your beliefs. I love you and probably always will. But I can't help you unless you let me. John tried to help you remember who you are. You sent him away, back to the reservation. Now when I try to help you, you push me away. By not being totally honest with me. I am the reality. You have been so caught up in the illusions of your past, you can't see the realities of the present. Your actions will destroy you. And they will destroy us. Maybe we were not meant to be. Maybe we have both been blind and stupid. It's obvious I was wrong about you."*

Maya walked into the kitchen and made some actions as if she cared about the dinner she was preparing. She didn't dare to look at Joseph. He hadn't moved. She knew he was looking at her. All she could think was, *'Please tell me you care and that you'll give it up. Give up the fight for the land. The fight you can't win. Give up the charade that you want to help the white man and his government.'*

But instead, she heard him move away. He walked toward his bedroom and closed the door behind him. Was that it? Did she handle it wrong? She told him it was over. And she didn't leave him any room or opening to come back. She felt like such a fool. She finished the dinner and ate it. But she didn't taste it. Eating was only a way of making time pass for her now. She lay down on the couch and cried herself to sleep.

CHAPTER 26

THE RECORDING

Maya heard sounds of water running. She had slept so soundly, she felt groggy and very nauseous. But her logical side kicked in and she knew she only had seconds to do what she must do.

By the time Joseph came out of the shower, she was in her room behind a closed door. The paper-thin disc – the latest in electronic spy technology – was safely attached to the inside front of his jacket lapel, and it was back in its position, lying ready for him on his bed.

As Maya listened to him moving around the apartment, she felt torn. Her emotional self wanted to run to him and tell him she loved him and believed in him, and that it didn't matter what he did. But she couldn't. Not now that she knew he had abandoned his beliefs and been won over by the political talent that surrounded him, feeding him lies. They had made him believe he could succeed and she knew he wanted to use them as much as they wanted to use him for their own ends. He was such a smart man, so charismatic and talented. But he wasn't the same man she thought she loved. She only could hope he'd see what was happening and leave it all behind him. If he did, and returned to the reservation, then she would follow him. To the ends of the earth.

Maya heard him leave. What was she going to do for all of those hours? How would she endure this waiting? She decided to sit and write a final report on the Hopi people. She didn't know what good it would do – it had gone way beyond his people to a political situation. But for her, this would be therapy. And she wanted to say something for the record.

She began, *"We've investigated a man named Joseph Pahana, a Hopi Indian, who wanted to change the world. He succeeded in saving many 'souls', but failed to accomplish his objectives. He became involved in political thoughts. Thoughts that didn't reflect Hopi beliefs. So we must separate him from his people. Our white man's society has succeeded in corrupting him. We must fault our own society for that.*

"We have not corrupted his small Hopi nation. We cannot fault the Hopi people for their beliefs. If we fault them, so must we fault Eastern mysticism. Hopi 'myth' closely parallels the Tantric teachings of Tibetan and Hindu mysticism – they elucidate the functions of man's centers and describe in full the stages of mankind's development. Western civilization views the psychic achievements of the East with a suspicious alarm comparable to that with which the East views our hydrogen bombs, interceptor missiles and space rockets."

She continued on with more on the Hopi belief and traditions as well as their affirmations serving the cosmic spirit of mankind and that of temporal man. Then she added, *"Our continent is in political chaos. We are currently geologically at risk. Could it hurt us to let them talk, or for us to listen? If we chose not to listen to them – then let us have the decency to leave them alone. We have no right to interfere with this ancient, strong people…Who can doubt the signs that a transition to another great new age has begun? Let them follow their beliefs. Let them prepare for their new World.*

"Don't fault the Hopi nation for our mistakes. Fault ourselves. And try to learn from it."

For whatever good it would do, at least Maya would have said her piece.

She checked her watch. It had only been two hours. How

much longer would she have to wait? She knew she must accept defeat – she had lost Joseph. Maya had nothing to stay here for. So she went to her room and started packing.

Thirty minutes later, she knew she couldn't wait alone. She went to see Tanner and wait with him.

"Why is it I'm not surprised?" He asked when he looked up from his desk and saw her. *"Okay, we can wait together. No problem. Why don't you sit down before you fall down?"*

She dropped her report on his desk and sat down.

"What is this?"

"My final report – I wanted to go on record about a few things. Don't look worried, I don't talk about any plots. You can read it if you want. Besides, I'm sure that after the surveillance team returns, you won't need me on this case anymore."

After reading it, Tanner looked up at her with a slow smile, *"You like these Hopi people, don't you? Could I ask you a personal question, hypothetically, of course?"*

"Sure, you can ask. I may answer it, I may not…"

"If Joseph Pahana walked away from all this and became a simple Indian again, would you walk away with him?"

"Yes, I would."

"I knew you'd say that." He rose from his desk, needing to look away from her, out the window. To look at something, anything, somewhere. He felt some kind of pain deep inside him. What had he really expected from her, anyway? He had never been any good at the *'game called love'*. And he played it especially bad with her. Played it? He had never even approached her about it. His feelings would have to stay buried inside him. He took a moment to mentally congratulate Joseph Pahans, who wasn't playing the game well, either. She deserved so much more

than what she was getting. And what was she getting? Nothing. Maybe in time. He would wait, again. In time, maybe there would be a chance.

The wait turned out to be a long one. They filled the time with a long lunch at Tanner's desk. Maya found it difficult to eat, her stomach was upset. She ended up eating all the antacid tablets in her bag, along with all that Tanner had.

Finally, the surveillance team returned, and Tanner stood holding an audio tape in his hands. They sat down and listened to it all. Maya let most of it pass through her mind, not registering. But certain parts were hard for her to ignore. Joseph appeared uneasy, with an uncertain, shaky voice. Gordon seemed to be reassuring everyone why they were meeting.

At one point, Joseph had approached Gordon, *"David, I really need to talk to you about something. I've been thinking, and..."*

Gordon was quick to interrupt him, *"Now, Joseph, don't do so much thinking. Remember this – we have been meeting for almost a year – from that day I heard your speech in Chicago and started talking with you, remember? Now, we have a lot to cover today – so please, Joseph, try to relax. And listen closely."*

Gordon's voice rose in volume, as he was supposedly addressing the entire group now. *"Let me remind us all why we are here. We need a new leader for President. And Joseph is our man. We have been training him for that day. Remember, Joseph, Congress can legislate, appropriate, investigate, deliberate, terminate, and educate – all essential functions. But Congress is not organized to initiate, negotiate, or act with the kind of swift and informal discretion that our changing world so often requires. Leadership can come only from the Presidency."* Several voices called out Joseph's name.

The discussion continued to praise Joseph and how

Joseph is the one to give strength and confidence to the American people, and how this group will support him all the way. *"We will get you the political consensus. Consensus has never meant unanimity. There have been no policies in this office that have not had dissent. We will help you get broad agreement on your planned principles of conduct. We will invent new domestic and foreign policies, economic and military policies that will light a fire under those we need to support you. You will have a coalition. And after you are elected, you can save this world, save those souls. As agreed, your political theme will be 'Project Redesign – the Age of Cooperation.'"* There were the sounds of various voices in the background agreeing.

As the discussion continued, they reviewed lobbying objectives, financial objectives, expansion of global influence, concluding with their request for Joseph to continue to trust them. *"We have spent months isolated from our jobs, our families, preparing ourselves for now. For you."*

There was a pause, and Joseph gave David Gordon what he was waiting to hear, *"Yes, I know. And I appreciate that. I am here."*

Maya felt like crying. Joseph had given up – he had let them talk him into staying with them and their ridiculous plan. She didn't want to hear anymore, but couldn't seem to stop listening.

The discussion turned to raising donations and how donors will want influence. They talked about how party loyalty has been replaced by identification with interest groups, how power has been transferred from party to lobby. They reassured Joseph about how they will guide him every step of the way, and how they will slowly begin the changes that he wants.

Occasionally Joseph would ask a question to clarify an action or policy that was being discussed, as well as how to handle the media, where Ted Knowles as press agent joined the conversation explaining how to understand the ways the media worked and the bureaucracy worked.

Joseph still appeared to lack real interest in the discussions, seemed more to be acting out a role expected of him. *"This is all amazing. There is so much work to be done to change things for the better. But we can't start right away, we have to use people in the meantime. It all seems so against what I believe in. But, I guess I don't have much choice, do I?"*

Gordon reacted with a flat *"No. We struck a bargain. Now we are in the middle of making it all happen. It's too late. You'll just have to trust us, Joseph."*

There followed a long silence. Apparently, the meeting for this day was over. *"Joseph, I think we've done quite well today. I think that's it for now, gentlemen. See you tomorrow,"* says Gordon. As you could hear voices slowly moving away to leave, Gordon made one more effort, *"Joseph, remember what I've said. And we won't discuss it again, okay?"*

Tanner turned off the tape, *"It won't be long, and the President and Attorney General will put an end to this. Gordon and Pinkerton are fucked. And so is Joseph, Maya."*

"I've got to warn him, Elliott."

"I think it may be too late for that. And if he's smart, he'll know it. The best thing he could do is call the Attorney General and tell her there's a plot and confess it all. Then maybe they'll let him live. I mean it, Maya, or his days will be numbered."

Tanner rose from his chair, *"I have to go. My Director is waiting for this tape. Will you be okay?"*

Maya looked pale, *"No, I don't think I'll ever be okay again."*

CHAPTER 27

THE WHITE HOUSE

Several blocks away, Joel Wattenberg was pacing in front of the President's desk, listening intently to the phone in his ear. He frowned, then closed his eyes, then glared at the President as if to say, '*Bad news, Chief. Really bad news.*'

The President was holding a letter and peered at Wattenberg over his reading glasses, while Joel pacing back and forth like Der Fuhrer really was irritating to him and he made a mental note to say something about it.

Wattenberg slammed the phone down. And continued pacing, "*Whatever.*" He sat in a chair across the desk and folded his hands under his chin. He was very deep in thought, and the President tried to ignore him.

Suddenly Wattenberg slapped the desk, and bolted to his feet, making the President jump, "*Jesus!*"

Joel moped to the windows, sulking for awhile and stared through the glass. Then he began pacing again, but much slower now. He was still painfully in thought.

The President tried to ignore Wattenberg, which wasn't easy. What helped was that he was feeling good. The country was experiencing more natural disasters every day. But it was a wonderful crisis. The ratings were back up, with his image clean and polished and America feeling pretty good about itself because he was in command. He felt sure the reelection next year was in the bag.

Wattenberg grabbed the phone, calling several people,

repeating the same message. At last, he looked at the President, *"I've called an emergency meeting."* The President went back to his letters. He was never a curious type. Joel would inform him in time what the emergency was.

Soon, the Oval Office was full of somber faces. As usual, Wattenberg ran the meeting. *"We might have a problem. It is in our best interests to have Joseph Pahana as opposition for the election. But it looks like the man is thinking of backing out. We want to have a plan ready, so we can feed the media to our advantage if this man does get popsicle toes."* He walked to the window, looking through the glass for a moment, in deep thought. Turning around, he returned to the conversation, *"Suppose, just suppose, we can make out that this Indian, who may be on the verge of causing our greatest national crisis, was dirty? I mean, we could make him look dirty, even evil. Evil intentions. That's it – he was the one courting the opposition. He wants the motherlode for himself, and all the publicity that goes with it. Selfish interests. Indian interests. We kill off his faked-up good character and make his party look bad for even talking seriously with him. It's done all the time."*

The President was frowning, then seemed to see the point. *"Ah, yes. We share the information with the media because we've got to save the country we love from being ruined. If it looks like he wants out, shouldn't we do this before it happens? After the fact, we wouldn't look so good, right?"*

The DCI agreed, *"I think we ought to do this immediately. I really don't think the man will last much longer. He's beginning to develop a conscience. We want to stay one step ahead in this election – otherwise, we're out of business. Capisce?"*

Everyone seemed to agree. Attorney General Levin-Gallagher added, *"A logical conclusion, Pinky. Look, we've agreed before about the Indians. They knew that if their fantasies, dreams of being recognized and reimbursed, were acted on, it might lead to disaster. Better their loss than ours. So, they lose their 'Savior'.*

187

So what? We lost ours once, and we've existed for another 2,000 years."

The President seemed thoughtful, *"We've got to manipulate the media just right and not overplay this."* He continued on, sharing his insight with his associates, as Wattenberg waited for him to finish. He would stay quiet for a few minutes. It was important to allow the President to take charge occasionally.

When the President was done, he cracked a joke and they all laughed. But Pinkerton seemed concerned. *"What if this guy really is a holy man?"*

"That's irrelevant," responded the President.

"Quite correct."

"Besides, if this guy is really some sort of 'holey-moley', then let this glass of ice water turn into chocolate milk." As he sat his glass back on the desk, all eyes in the room stared at the glass, as if expecting a change. Then they laughed again.

And the discussion continued, as they outlined a possible media release. After about ten minutes, the President reached for his ice water glass. There was a loud scream and the sound of breaking glass, as he threw his glass down on the floor. Everyone was still as they watched the brown liquid form a stain on the ancient oriental rug.

The President turned to look at Wattenberg, *"What the hell have you done?"*

Silence, everywhere. Until Wattenberg responded, *"No one touch it."*

The President's face was reddening and sweating, *"This is NOT funny!"*

No one said a word.

"The man is a demon," the President jumped up from his desk, sending papers flying. *"Only an evil being could do that. I want him dead. Out of our lives. Before I go nuts. Joel…"* Everyone stared at their leader, thinking about what he'd said. Like most who had never faced battle, they found embarrassment and death unattractive.

"Don't worry, Mr. President. I'll take care of everything." Wattenberg waved the others from the room. *"Let the dust settle first, Chief, before we do anything. We're all in shock."* But he was thinking, *'The ill-born are generally prone to emotional outbursts like that.'*

As he began wiping the sweat from his face, the President began taking the first step to his own destruction. *"Eliminate the cause, you eliminate the result."*

"Your point, sir?"

"Do it, Joel."

"Please, Chief. We're all a little stressed here. We can't just terminate someone for doing what he may not even realize he did. Besides, you know the rules. Termination with extreme prejudice of civilians, we need direct orders from you, cosigned by the Chairman of the Joint Chiefs and the DCI."

"Joel, nothing in writing. I want him dead. Just arrange it."

"As you wish, Chief."

CHAPTER 28

THE APARTMENT

At first, Maya thought the apartment was empty when she got there. It was so dark and quiet. She reached for the light switch, turning on the living room overhead light, and was startled to see Joseph just sitting there.

"What are you doing here in the dark? You scared me."

"Sorry." He just sat staring at her. *"I saw your packed suitcases. You meant it, didn't you? You're really going to leave."*

"Yes, tonight. Unless you do something."

"I don't know what more I can say or do."

Looking at him, Maya couldn't give up. She walked over, kneeling on the floor, taking Joseph's hands in hers. *"Stop this charade, Joseph. Before it's too late."*

"I can't do that."

"You have to."

"You don't understand, Maya. This country, these people, need me."

"I need you, Joseph. I need you alive and well. You won't survive this. It won't work anymore."

"Yes, it will work. It has to. This is the only chance I have to reach all of the people."

"No, you aren't facing reality. Joseph, I love you. Come

back to the reservation with me. Your people need you. If you stay, you won't succeed."

"I have to try. I have a responsibility."

"But it won't work. You will never make it. You'll never be President. I heard a tape of your meeting today. The Party is using you, Joseph. Their plan won't work. You have to quit – now. I'll help you do it. Please let me."

He looked at her questioningly. Did what she said register with him, about hearing the tape? *"I can't, Maya. I made a promise. I just can't quit this. Over two centuries and fifty elections. Americans have been complaining about the nature of presidential campaigns and candidates. From the founding of this nation, Americans have wanted a leader who is simultaneously a man OF the people and a man ABOVE the people. Now, they'll get one. I just need to get elected. And then I can continue my work to save the world."*

"But Joseph, don't you see? This whole charade is a broad assault on the nation's soul? You are acting completely against what you believe. You have become corrupt."

"It's too late to pull out."

"Even when they're going to kill the current President? Joseph, wake up, or you'll go down with them."

"You don't know what you're talking about. And they do."

Maya got up and began walking around the room, not knowing how to reach this man without coming right out and telling him she had been *'spying'* on him. *"There's nothing I can say to dissuade you?"*

He shook his head no, looking at the floor instead of at her.

"So, Joseph, instead of being a spiritual leader of the people, you want to become a political leader. You're going to

mortgage the presidency with a series of pledges – that you can't activate."

Joseph just sat there, not responding, not moving. Not even looking at her. She had to do something. Maybe she should tell him the truth. That may shock him into reality.

"Wake up, Joseph. The President will hear the tapes. Listen to me," she knelt down again, reached up and took his head in her hands, forcing him to look at her face. *"I work for the F.B.I. I heard all the tapes we have from surveillance, everything, the speech that you thought was too harsh, about the media relations 'make-believe' program, about the five-point military plans. All of it. As well as Gordon's statement about getting rid of the President. And the President will listen to these tapes soon. It's over, the whole plan is ended. Gordon will never work with a President again. The others will be reabsorbed back into their jobs, and it will all be hidden.*

"Go to the President and the Attorney General. Tell them you didn't know until today what they had planned. Ask them for their forgiveness and promise them you won't get involved in the political world again. That's the only way you can save yourself. Listen to me, Joseph, your role as candidate is all over. Don't you understand? I work for the government…I know."

"I don't believe you. You're lying, just to get me to stop. You're an Anthropologist, not an F.B.I. spy. I don't believe you, Maya. Stop lying to me."

"I'm not lying, Joseph. You have to believe me."

"I can't believe you. If I do, then that means that you and I are a lie. That you didn't care. I can't believe that."

Maya stood up, looking down at him, like a teacher about to reprimand a student, hands on her hips. *"Listen to me, Joseph. This is the truth. I occasionally help the F.B.I with Native American problems. I also am an Anthropologist at the Museum. And I happen to love you. If you can't believe me, then you are doomed. You won't save the world, you can't even save yourself, unless you listen to me."*

Joseph was staring at her and rose from his seat so that they were standing face to face, close enough that she could feel the heat from his body. She also saw the rage on his face, *"I can't listen to any more of this."* He moved past her and out the front door of the apartment.

At first, she couldn't believe he just left her, without even giving her a chance. By the time she followed him outside, she couldn't see him anywhere on the street. Then she saw a car moving past, a plain unmarked black one. Tanner's agents??

This all meant he was gone. It was over. He had left her behind, not believing in her. She had just talked to a doomed man. Her heart felt sick, she felt nauseated she was so sick at heart.

Maya stood in the middle of his apartment, wondering what to do. What could she do? Nothing. Now she had to think of herself. She had better leave, before he returned. If something happened to change his mind, he knew where to find her in Boston.

But she had to let him know that he could find her there, if he wanted. That she still cared and would leave a door open for him. She decided to leave him a note.

"My beloved Joseph,

Finley Peter Dunne's Mr. Dooley observed long ago, 'Americans build their triumphal arches out of bricks – so that we will have something handy to hurl at our heroes when they invariably disappoint us.'

No, I won't stay here to hurl the first brick. I saw you as a hero – for all of us. You have disappointed me, Joseph. So I must leave. I can't stay and watch you fall.

I'm returning home to Boston and pray you will follow me.

I love you, Maya"

CHAPTER 29

LEAVING

Joseph returned to his apartment a few hours later. While walking around the huge city, he realized just what he was losing by listening to the white men around him. His spirits. His beliefs. Maya. When he saw the note she had left, he knew what he must do. He packed just what he needed. Then, he wrote two notes. One to David Gordon, telling him to find another candidate. The other to Maya. He left the apartment without even looking back. He had somewhere to go. He didn't notice the two men sitting silently in the car parked down the block.

The next day, Joel Wattenberg received a call from David Gordon. *"He's done it. He quit on us. All of our brilliant plans, down the tubes."* Apparently, there was more collusion crossing over the party lines than previously apparent. There was a larger plan in place, and Joel seemed to be in charge of it.

Wattenberg sighed, *"Yeah, I know, David. So, we'll come up with someone else. Relax. Leave it to me. You worry too much."*

"What do I tell the others? We've spent a whole year on this, for God's sake."

"Tell them to wait until you hear back from me."

"Can we just let him walk like this?"

"We let him walk. I've got everything covered. You'll never hear from him again. No one will."

CHAPTER 30

BOSTON

When she got home to Boston, Maya stayed in bed for an entire day. Exhausted and sick physically and emotionally. When she finally felt strong enough to get up, she collected her mail. It had been two days since she came home. She didn't feel up to looking through the huge pile of envelopes.

Maybe a visit to her office in the Museum would distract her. She spent a long day writing research papers on pre-Columbian artifacts, cataloging items from shipments, and designing new artifact displays. But she couldn't get Joseph out of her mind.

She tried to call him. Then she called Elliott Tanner. She had to know what was happening.

"I've been worried about you, Maya," he seemed actually glad to hear from her.

"If you were so worried, why didn't you call me?"

"Because I felt I had to wait for you to call me. Have you heard from him? Joseph, I mean?"

"What do you mean, have I heard from him? Why should I have?"

"No one else has. He's dropped out of sight. I thought maybe he would have contacted you."

"Wait a minute. When did he drop out of sight?"

"That night – the same day we listened to the tape. What happened, Maya? What did you tell him?

"I told him that I'd heard his tapes, that it would soon be over for him. I asked him to confess it all to the President and the Attorney General. He refused. And he wouldn't believe me."

"Jesus, no wonder he disappeared. He must have believed you, whether he really wanted to or not."

"Tanner, can't we find him? I mean, can't you? Please, I need to know where he is. I have something important to tell him."

"We're trying to. I know my two men are trailing him. At least I hope so. I haven't heard from them. I do know he didn't return to the reservation. He contacted David Gordon and backed out of if. We did search his apartment. All that's gone is an overnight bag and some clothes."

"Did you see my note to him? Was it still there?"

"No, we didn't find a note from anyone. He must have taken it with him."

"Now, think hard, Elliott. There was a small earthenware clay pot with a feather on a table in his living room. Was that gone?"

"Wait a minute, let me look at the inventory sheet we made." There was a slight pause. *"I don't see that listed. He must have taken that. Why? Was it important?"*

"Only to him."

"Maya, do you have any ideas where he may have gone?"

"If I did, and you found him, what would happen next?"

"I don't know. We'd have to let the Attorney General know. Then – I really don't know. Maybe it's better if we don't find him,

Maya."

"Tanner, I have a really big favor to ask of you."

"No, Maya. I know what you're going to ask me. Please, don't ask me that."

"How do you know what I'm going to ask?"

"I know you."

"Please, Elliott."

"Okay, go ahead. Ask it."

"Find him. For me. I can't go look myself. I'm a wreck physically. Guess all this has really stressed out my body. Find him, but don't let anyone know until I can see him. Please. I really need to talk with him first."

"If I can pull it off, I will. I promise."

"If he contacted Gordon, then the conspiracy must have been called off. But they are still guilty – why hasn't there been anything in the newspapers?"

"What do you want from me, a lesson on political media games?"

"Maybe, Elliott. I don't really understand how it all works, except what we heard on that tape."

"Okay, let me add just a little here. Remember how the Gulf of Tonkin incident was used to punish North Vietnam and to show L.B.J.'s toughness in the midst of a Presidential campaign? In the past, policies had been generally formed by government officials to respond to events, or to anticipate events and crises. Well, that event shows you how we have now reached the point where events are shaped to fit politics.

"Even when the facts about an event are reported

accurately by the government, the event may only be used as a justification for actions already decided on. Where government controls access to both events and documents, information becomes a commodity, a tool of policy. It is shaped and packaged by the government and sold to the public through the media.

"Right now, the current administration is most likely holding off on using any information on Gordon or the Party until it can be better used – like after the Party announces their new candidate, which of course won't be Joseph anymore. You can bet the administration will distort as much as possible to hurt the Party, making them look dishonest as hell! Of course, the truth seems to be strong enough to do that. It'll be the timing. They're waiting until the right moment, that's all."

"What about the American people's right to know?"

Tanner laughed. *"There have been instances where governmental figures have agreed that, 'It is believed that as a general principle, the people don't have a right to know the truths in government.' Does that give you an idea how our government feels about the American public being told? Just remember, Maya, in the crucial field of national security, the government controls almost all the important channels of information. There is a greater possibility that information will either not be distributed, or that it will be distorted. Don't expect to read the truth about any of this in your newspaper."*

"Okay, listen, Tanner, I've been trying to think. I really don't know where Joseph may have gone. All I know is that he has lost his spiritual link."

"What? Please speak normally, if you don't mind."

"I'm sorry. You see, the Hopi way is to think about family, friends and village matters. Such problems as world-wide events, like war and politics, are considered destructive and not to be thought about. Joseph had stopped listening to tradition, had

wandered too far from home and family, losing his way. His spirit world had another destiny planned for him. So, they abandoned him. I think he has gone somewhere that is on high ground, that has no people around, just land and sky. I think he has gone in search of the spirits. That's all I can figure."

"Jesus, Maya, that really narrows it down."

"Elliott, I know I'm not much help. But please know, I'm trying."

"All right. I'll be back in touch. If you hear from him, call me, okay?"

"No, I won't do that, Elliott. I can't do that."

"Damnation, girl! You want my help, but you won't help me?"

"I can't. I don't think you could understand."

Tanner was quiet for a moment. Then, in a very quiet voice, he said, *"Give me more credit than that. I DO understand, Maya. You love him. I guess I shouldn't be surprised you said that. I'm just not used to such honesty. Thanks for that anyway."*

"Will you still…"

"Yeah, I promise. Will you be okay?"

"No, not really. But I'll survive. I have to."

"Yeah, you're a survivor all right. Just remember I care about you, survivor, okay?"

"Thanks Elliott. Goodbye."

Maya couldn't have felt worse, either physically or mentally. And, she didn't need a doctor to know what was wrong – it was more than just a broken heart – much more.

She decided to have a cup of hot tea and read the paper, searching for the latest news on the disasters along the Ring of Fire. The volcanic activity forming the stepping stone islands had apparently abated for awhile. But there seemed to be more disasters.

There were floods, it would seem, everywhere. Brazil, France, China, Pakistan, and in the middle of the U.S. Even Chicago was completely under water again, the Great Lakes were overflowing. And killer tornadoes in Illinois, Kansas and Oklahoma.

And this new viral strain with more than a half million dead in the U.S., five million dead in India and two million in Africa so far. The newspaper told Maya that there were only two other rivals in history – the Plague of Justinian's reign and the 14th Century Black Death. And there were earthquakes around the world that were increasing in frequency and intensity.

So, that's it, thought Maya. The world is ending. No one has ever seen so much disaster in the world at one time. But what to do? Was there anything Maya could do? Was there any safe place to go?

It was time to check her mail, even though it didn't seem very important to her then. But it would help pass the time. She began making separate piles for bills and throwing away the junk mail when she saw the envelope, recognizing Joseph's handwriting. She tore it open.

"My dearest Maya…The hopes we had were good dreams. They didn't work out, but I'm glad we had them. I need to find my spirits again. I am like a 'hollow soul' – searching for promise and fulfillment, but empty of hope.

All the speeches I shared with so many – they have just become words without meaning anymore. I have lost all meaning to my life. How can I save others when I can no longer save myself?

> *You were right. I shall always love you…Joseph"*

Joseph, where are you??

CHAPTER 31

MEXICO

"You'd better not drink that water," Niehardt had snuck up behind Weatherford, succeeding in scaring the wits out of him.

"What are we doing here, anyway? I mean, I've always wanted to visit Mexico, see the ruins and all. But we can't even act like tourists. We have to hide and even follow these guys off into the jungle." Weatherford swatted at his head, *"I swear I'm gonna get malaria from all these mosquitos."*

"Well, we're almost done on this assignment. I reached Wattenberg and we have our instructions. It has become like a military situation, pal. Do as I tell you and follow me. We have a job to do."

John Saxon stood beside Joseph, atop a large ruin that resembled a pyramid. *"Thank you for contacting me, Joseph, and asking me to meet you here."*

"I needed you to come and see our old ancestral home with me, John. I have found the spirits again. And, they have told me our future. It is here, in our past, here in this Mayan Old Empire."

"Welcome back to us, my brother."

They stood side by side, surveying the ruins. This small village grew to be a large city, a great cultural and religious center. It was built in three sections, completely surrounded by a high wall. On the ground floor, the kachinas taught the initiates the history and meaning of the three previous worlds and the purpose of the fourth world. They were also taught the structure and functions of the human body, with the highest function of the mind to understand the great spirit world working within man. The workings of the planetary system came into play, about how the stars affect the climate, crops and man himself. They learned about the '*open door*' on top of their heads, how to keep it open and converse with the Creator.

John and Joseph could feel the presence of the spirits and knelt to open their kopavis in prayer.

The movements were swift and silent. John and Joseph never heard the agents sneak up behind them. And they didn't have the time to feel much pain. It was over quickly.

Agents Niehardt and Weatherford left the ruins and forest behind them, hardly speaking to one another as they drove their Jeep beyond the town near Chiapas, Mexico. Niehardt was the first to break the long silence, "*There's supposed to be an air strip here somewhere,*" as he glanced at his watch. "*We should just be on time to meet the helicopter Wattenberg said he'd send for us.*"

Weatherford felt confused, "*Why, Ralph? Why did we have to do it?*"

"*Because it was our job. They tell us to do something, we just do it. I just don't understand the significance of slitting their throats. Wattenberg said it was the Sioux way of assassinating. But what does it matter? No one's going to care, anyway. How is the next group of tourists going to know that? Well, I guess, maybe it is a fitting death for an Indian. Here we are…*"

Soon after they were airborne, there was a strange smell on the copter. The pilot showed Niehardt how to hold the copter controls as he disappeared in the back. The smoke appeared at the same time Weatherford noticed the pilot jumping out. "*What the…*"

A roar passed through their ears as the helicopter and their bodies exploded. Then it became quiet as small pieces drifted down over the jungle, falling like raindrops to feed the lush growth below.

CHAPTER 32

BOSTON

Maya sat at her kitchen table with only a hot cup of tea for company. It was dark and gloomy. So was her mood. When a light knock sounded at her back door, she hoped it would be Joseph. It wasn't.

It was Elliott Tanner, and his face looked flushed. *"You've got to get out of here! Grab only what you really need. I've got to get you away – now!!"*

"What is it? What's going on? Tanner, tell me!"

"In a minute. Now, move!"

She grabbed a pair of jeans, couple of t-shirts, a sweatshirt jacket, a change of underwear, and her kachina doll. When she came back downstairs, she grabbed her purse and followed Tanner back out the rear door.

"Where are we going?"

"Shhh!! Just shut up for awhile and stay with me," he whispered.

As they followed the shadowed, dark backyards, avoiding lighted areas, she realized something terrible must have happened and her life must be in danger.

Tanner pointed ahead, for her to get in a rental car, parked several blocks from the house in someone's quiet, dark driveway. He drove down the street and around the corner before even turning on the headlights.

Maya sat staring at him, catching her breath, and trying to wait as patiently as she could for him to tell her what was happening. This was the first time she had really felt like a spy, sneaking around in shadows. And she was very frightened.

Tanner's profile showed that he was, too. Finally, he seemed to have his thoughts organized. He reached into his jacket inside pocket and handed her an envelope. He turned his face to look at her for a second, and she saw a look she had never seen there before. A look of sorrow, but yet a look of tenderness.

"Open the envelope, Maya."

Inside, she saw several hundred dollars, all in twenties, and a one-way airline ticket. The ticket was to Flagstaff, Arizona.

"What is this, Elliott? And why the secrecy? I even left the lights on in my house."

"Good. They'll think you're still there."

"Who?"

He didn't answer her.

"Elliott Tanner. Either you tell me what is going on or stop this car and let me out. Who will still think I'm at home?"

"I'm not sure. Someone."

"Someone who?"

"A lot has happened, Maya. And your life may be in danger."

"Whoa! Wait a minute! Please tell me what is going on. And why am I in danger? I work for the government. Don't they know that?"

"That doesn't matter anymore. You are too involved and

know too much. To some people you may be expendable."

"Don't they realize that I pledged loyalty to my country? I took a vow, Elliott, just like you did. I am NOT expendable!"

"I'm sorry, Maya. I couldn't take a chance. I just couldn't let anything happen to you. I care for you, Maya, more than you will ever know. I had to do something to keep you safe. But you can't come back here for awhile. You have to go to Arizona. You need to go to the reservation."

"Why the Hopi Reservation?"

"Because you love those people. And they love you. And will hide you."

"Elliott, this ticket is not in my name."

"I know. Please play it my way."

She kept looking at the ticket. *"Is this a real person? This Eileen Raines?"*

"Yes," and for the first time he smiled, a little. *"I had a crush on her in high school. It's the only name I could think of with no connection to either you or me."*

"There's something else, Elliott, that you're not telling me. How come all of a sudden do I need to disappear? And why so quickly?"

"Because they got to him. And now they may be coming to get you."

"What do you mean 'got to him'? Who? Joseph?"

"Yes."

"Elliott," she turned her body to face him, *"tell me he's all right. That he's alive and will be able to meet me in Arizona."*

"No."

"No, what? Do you mean not now?"

"Not now. Not ever."

"Elliott, tell me. Please tell me what happened. What kind of danger was he in?"

"The worst kind."

"What did they do to him? I need to know."

"We think we know who's responsible. We can't prove it yet. But we will." He looked at her profile, knowing she was preparing herself for the bad news. *"We had two agents watching him, following him. But they didn't report directly to me. They received instructions from someone in the President's administration. We think he was heading up the coup against his own boss. Well, he gave his instructions. And four men died. Just like that. The two agents, John Saxon and Joseph. I'm sorry, Maya. I couldn't be sure, but as soon as I heard, I made plans to get you out. Before we can build the case and take action, you may be in danger. For knowing too much. They couldn't be sure of your loyalties."*

She couldn't speak. She couldn't even breathe. Maya put her hand on her chest and pushed, as if to make sure her heart kept beating, and to push air out of her lungs. And then when she breathed back in, she moaned.

"Maya, listen to me. You can mourn for him later. Right now, you have to concentrate on escape."

She knew he was right, but right now she wanted to die, too. *"You bastard!"*

"No, Maya. Not me. Them!"

"But you're one of them. If they told YOU to kill someone

for the supposed good of the country, you would have. You're just as bad as they are."

"If it'll help you to hate me, Maya, then go ahead. Hate me."

Now she believed. She believed in everything the Hopi People had told her. She believed that Joseph was a true prophet. And that he failed both his people and his spirits. Now, she understood. And she knew she must be with his people.

"You're right, Elliott. Now I need to concentrate. So, for awhile, I am Miss Eileen Raines. Thank you for the ticket and the money. Thank you for caring."

"It was easy, Maya."

They had arrived at the airport. *"I'll just drop you off up here. I think it's best I don't get out. If anyone sees me, they may recognize you."*

So this was it, the end of their eight-year association. Maya reached over, pulling Tanner's face to hers and gave him a sweet, sisterly kiss. *"I'll never forget you, Elliott."*

And then she left the car, not looking back.

CHAPTER 33

ARIZONA

It was dark. Maya stood on the mesa ledge overlooking the Painted Desert, watching for the new dawn. Everyone had welcomed her back the day before, as if she had been expected. There had been a letter from Joseph waiting for her here. Maya could feel his folded letter in her pocket and reread the message in her mind.

"My dearest Maya…If my death occurs, as has been prophecized, you must take my people to a safe haven. Return my people, now our people, to the Red House, or Palatkwapi, the Red City of the South, built by the Kachinas to be landmark of all clans in their migrations.

"I have sent a message to our Kachina spirits at Nuva tuky'ovi (San Francisco Peaks). The Kachina people are now at Palatkwapi – preparing it for our people. Look for Eototo, Aholi, Hehewuti and Cha'kwaina especially, who were there for us before. Many have said that the great Red City of the South was at Casa Grandes in Chihuahua, Mexico. Those 237 acres were indeed occupied by our people. But, that is not the safe haven I speak of.

"You will find Palatkwapi where it has always been. It has become known by specialists such as you as the Mayan Old Empire, Palenque. It is there, on that site, in Chiapas, Mexico, that the Kachinas await your arrival.

"Your father knew this place well. He knew that someday it

would play an important part in all our lives, especially yours. He would be proud of you.

"The spirits have told me that you will have a son – our son. And he will lead our Chosen People in the Fifth World. Remember me to him – don't let him forget that his father tried to please the spirits and his people.

"Take our people home. Tell our son of all you know. And remember me, always....Your Loving Joseph"

Kwa'gnwa mana appeared quietly beside Maya with a package for her. It was heavy, wrapped in a square, checkered blanket. *"This was Joseph's baby blanket. Look inside."*

Maya unwrapped it carefully, setting the blanket carefully aside, holding up what could only be a tiponi, about ten inches high, carved from sandstone. The figure appeared to be squatting, arms raised up from the elbows, knees bent, and legs extended out to the sides. The feet looked like bear claws. The head was large and round. There was no neck, just a slight indentation all around. On the stomach was painted in blue – the Nakwach symbol – a curved arc, like an upside-down smile, and another arc below to one side, like a happy-face smile.

"This is what the leader of our Bear Clan always has in his possession. It is for you to carry now – as our leader. It is now your responsibility to lead our people to our destination. You must be the first one to arrive there – and you must find a place for this fetish to sit. If there is a kiva there, that would be the place. And we shall continue using it for our ceremonies." Then, she smiled at Maya and walked away.

Maya once again stood on this mesa ledge, what Joseph had called *'the ceiling of the world'*. But this time, she was standing alone. Yet, somehow she felt no longer alone.

She realized she felt great love for these peaceful people and would be proud to lead them to Palatkwapi. She smiled, thinking how proud her father would be, just as Joseph had written. He always wanted her to continue his work, solving the riddle of the Mayan civilization. And here she was, going to a Mayan ruin to live with relatives of the Mayans.

The sun shone brightly overhead now, and Maya looked up to see an eagle overhead, who seemed to be calling out to her. She smiled up at him, wondering if he was saying something to her. Something, perhaps, like *"It's a good day to start a journey on the Hopi Road of Life."*

- THE BEGINNING -

AUTHOR'S NOTE

"There is no such thing as a little
country. The greatness of a people is
no more determined by their number than
the greatness of a man is determined
by his height."
…Victor Hugo

This novel is fiction but based on reality – the Hopi People of Arizona. These few Hopis, isolated for centuries on their remote mesas, have been a great people. Now their wheel of life is finally turning full circle. Their only hope is to take their place in the one great body of world humanity, translating their values into universal terms.

The history, and the hopes, of the Hopis lends us a perspective to see ourselves through uniquely indigenous American eyes. It shows us a people with immemorial tenure of their homeland and beliefs. The Hopis speak not as a defeated little minority in the richest and most powerful nation on earth, but with the rising voice of a people affirming their right to grow from their own native roots.

Our shallow rationalization cannot be permitted to discount as primitive nonsense any aspect of Hopi mysticism and symbolism. They sought in the white man their long-lost white brother, the mythical Pahana, and projected on us the sublimity of him who would establish at last the universal pattern of creation.

The coming of Pahana, the return of the Maya's bearded white god Kukulcan, the Toltecan and Aztecan Quetzalcoatl, is a myth of deep significance to all the Americas. It is the unfulfilled longing of all humanity.

Man's religious beliefs bring him strength. But must we rely on a higher level of perception rather than on political and economic expediencies to lead us out of our present world crisis? Is this too much, or too late, to hope for?

There are many satirical writings here about our American government which are fictionalized. This is all in keeping with the tone of the story. It by no means represents any legitimate considerations used to dishonor our government, but to add to this fictional representation. It is the individual citizen who has the freedom of opinion whether to criticize or applaud our government and its representatives. Those expressed here are not representative of my own, as the author.

Marilyn AUTHOR

OTHER BOOKS BY THE AUTHOR

Published Short Stories

"Beyond", Tales of Life, Mystery and Murder
"Reflexions", Lessons Learned Along Life's Journey
"Beyond 2", Strange But True Short Stories

Published History Books

"Our Roots Run Deep", the wRightSide Family History
    (A Genealogy Research Book)

To Be Published (over next three years)

"Murder on the Mesa" a Hightower Mystery
"The Knowing Tree", The Story of a Witness To History
"The Faces of Murder", a Hightower Mystery
"Murder on Trial", a Hightower Mystery
"A Question of Murder", a Hightower Mystery
"Murder on High", a Hightower Mystery

ABOUT THE AUTHOR

 **Marilyn Wright Dayton** has been writing all her life, from the time she could hold a pencil. Her life and career focused on the world of advertising in many roles. She was one of the originators of some of the more unique marketing vehicles in the nation over the years.

As an innovator in the new world of women and leadership, she has proven to create peak performances in startups, small business and non-profits. From the beginning of her career at the age of 12 as a radio quiz kid, she has been both in front of the camera and behind the camera as a fashion model, radio and TV show host and program producer. She holds degrees in marketing and business as well as in journalism. Over the past several decades, she has also been a newspaper reporter, creative writer, ad director, entrepreneur, consultant, trainer and an authority in the areas of creative marketing and top-notch business performance.

Through those years, her first loves have continued to be creative writing and art. She brings that to her research for her family's genealogy book *"Our Roots Run Deep",* available on Amazon. Her published books of short stories are also available on Amazon. She is at work on several novels in addition to *"The Hollow Soul".* You can read her blog at *www.FromGlam2Gram.com.*

Marilyn is now retired from the business world and makes her home with her family in Mystic, CT.

www.MarilynDayton.com
maredayt@yahoo.com

The Hollow Soul

Made in the USA
Middletown, DE
13 April 2021